I0533616

You Also May Enjoy These Books
by
Theodore Jerome Cohen

*Death by Wall Street**
*House of Cards (two editions)**
*Lilith**
*Night Shadows**
*Eighth Circle**
*Wheel of Fortune**
Frozen in Time†
Unfinished Business†
End Game†
Cold Blood††
Full Circle
The Hypnotist‡‡‡
Pepe Builds a Nest§
Rufus Finds a Home§
Fuzzy Wuzzy§
The Road Less Taken – Books 1 & 2
Creative Ink, Flashy Fiction – Books 1, 2, 3, 4, 5 & 6
Flash Fiction for Animal Lovers (Anthology Book 7)
Flash Fiction Stories of the Young (Anthology Book 8)
*Flash Fiction Stories of the Warrior (Anthology Book 9)***
*Flash Fiction Stories with a Feminine Twist (Anthology Book 10)***
*Flash Fiction Stories with a Masculine Twist (Anthology Book 11)***
*Flash Fiction Stories for the Religiously Inclined (Anthology Book 12)***
*Flash Fiction Stories for the Musically Inclined (Anthology Book 13)***
*Flash Fiction Stories of the Sea (Anthology Book 14)***
*Flash Fiction Stories for Students and Teachers (Anthology Book 15)***
*Flash Fiction Stories In Honor of Juneteenth (Anthology Book 16)***
*Flash Fiction Stories with Magical Realism (Anthology Book 17)***
*Flash Fiction Stories on Life and Death (Anthology Book 18)***

More Flash Fiction Stories for Animal Lovers (Anthology Book 19)**
Flash Fiction Stories On Love and Commitment (Anthology Book 20)**
Mementos (Anthology Books 1, 2, 3, 4, 5 & 6)
Death by Wall Street: The Screenplay
Beware Those Closest: The Screenplay
The Collected Works of Professor Emil Heisseluft§§

* A Detective Louis Martelli, NYPD, Mystery/Thriller
** Also contains short stories
† The Antarctic Murders Trilogy
†† The Antarctic Murders Trilogy (all three books)
‡ Young Adult (YA) novel written under the pen name "Alyssa Devine"
‡‡ Also available in a special paperback edition for readers with dyslexia
§ Illustrated childrens book in verse (K-3; *Pepe Builds a Nest* is available in English, Spanish, French, and Italian (English is the only book in verse))
§§ Communications/Electronics/Science humor written under the pen name "Professor Emil Heisseluft."

Visit us on the World Wide Web
http://www.theodore-cohen-novels.com
http://www.alyssadevinenovels.com

Martelli, NYPD

A Collection of Excerpts from the
Detective Louis "Lou" Martelli, NYPD,
Mystery/Thriller Series

Theodore Jerome Cohen

TJC Press

TJC Press
122 Shady Brook Drive
Langhorne, PA 19047-8027 USA
www.theodore-cohen-novels.com
© Theodore Jerome Cohen, 2023• All rights reserved

Without limiting the rights under the copyright reserved above, no part of this book may be reproduced, stored in or introduced into a retrieval system, or transmitted in any form or by any means—electronic, mechanical, photocopying, recording, or otherwise—without written permission from the author. The scanning, uploading, and distribution of this book via the Internet or any other means without written permission is punishable by law. Your support of the author's rights is appreciated.

The stories in this book are works of fiction, though some were inspired by real events. Except as noted in the **Endnotes**, which are made a part of this declaration, any resemblance to actual persons (living or dead), events, or locales in the context of the stories presented here, is coincidental. All brand names and product names used in this book are trademarks, registered trademarks, or trade names of their respective holders.

Some stories first appeared as submissions to Flash Fiction Challenges sponsored by Indies Unlimited (www.IndiesUnlimited.com); these were inspired by copyrighted photographic prompts provided by K.S. Brooks that were originally posted at Indies Unlimited.

First Edition; First Printing, 2023
ISBN: 9798379274412 (sc)

Published in the United States of America
Front cover design by Theodore Jerome Cohen
The paperback edition is printed using THE DOVES TYPE® typeface, Robert Green's digital recreation of the Doves Press Fount of Type. See **Endnote 1** for more information.
https://typespec.co.uk/doves-type/

Photo Credits
Front cover art: endomotion, Big Stock Photo
Frontispiece: Big Stock Photo
Photograph of Theodore Jerome Cohen: Susan Cohen, 2006
Photographic prompts copyrighted by K.S. Brooks are used with permission. The copyright or other attribution associated with any given photographic prompt (e.g., royalty-free acquisitions from Big Stock Photo; public domain; etc.) is provided with that prompt. Please provide documented proof of any errors or omissions in, or any changes requested to, these prompts (e.g., changes resulting from inadvertent copyright violations), by letter, to TJC Press.

eBook created by Kindle Direct Publishing (KDP)
Printed by KDP, An Amazon.com Company
Available from Amazon.com and other retail outlets

Because of the dynamic nature of the Internet, any Web addresses or links contained in this book may have changed since publication and may no longer be valid. The views expressed in this work are solely those of the authors.

To Chief Joe Bartorilla and Members of the
Middletown Township Police Department,
Langhorne, Pennsylvania

Thank you for your service.

■

"The world, even the smallest parts of it, is filled with things you don't know."

Sherman Alexi
The Absolutely True Diary of a Part-Time Indian

■

Table of Contents

A Note from Theodore Jerome Cohen

Beginning in 2010, and for five years thereafter, I penned several books, six to be exact, which I refer to as the Detective Louis "Lou" Martelli, NYPD, mystery/thriller series. They feature, as the protagonist, a veteran of the first Iraqi War who lost a leg when the Black Hawk helicopter on which he was the crew chief was shot down during the assault on that nation's capital. Under a special dispensation given to him by the mayor of New York City, and because his father had been a former street cop, Martelli was allowed to "sit" the exam for detective, which he passed. We first encounter him as a homicide detective investigating the horrific death of a Wall Street analyst, whose severed head is found spiked to the Wall Street Bull in New York's Financial District. The story is based on a true case of malfeasance by the Food and Drug Administration (FDA) in its rejection of a revolutionary new treatment for (in the book) breast cancer and the negligence of the Securities and Exchange Commission (SEC) in not investigating the collusion behind the FDA's action and the members of the financial community who had a vested interest in the failure of this treatment.

Other books in the series explore homicides tied to the financial collapse of 2008, corruption in New York City, real-life vampire cults, teen suicide, New York political corruption, and a New York mob's efforts to take over the trash hauling and recycling business in Lancaster, Pennsylvania . . . all stories based on real-life, so much so that some readers have difficulty separating fact from fiction!

An overview of the books is given at the end of this volume, where you also will find a list and brief description of many of the characters you will encounter in the six-book series. Some, such as Lou, Stephanie, and Missy, are based on people I know in my life. These characters have their real-life counterparts' characteristics, mannerisms, and "voices," which made writing dialogue both easy and fun.

Many had told me, following the publication of *Death by Wall Street*, I should see if it might be possible to have them made into movies. To that end, I created screenplays for both this novel as well as for *House of Cards*. The screenplay for the latter was titled *Beware Those Closest*. Despite hiring both a professional screenplay editor and a Hollywood agent, there was (as they say) "no joy in Mudville." Still, I cite these screenplays here for completeness.

Finally, with respect to the six Martelli novels, please know they can be read in any order. Don't be afraid to jump in at any point!

People ask me: "Why do you use photographic prompts when you write short stories and flash fiction?" Larry Sultan, an American photographer from the San Fernando Valley in California, provides one answer: "Photography is there to construct the idea of us as a great family and we go on vacations and take these pictures and then we look at them later and we say, 'Isn't this a great family?' So photography is instrumental in creating family not only as a memento, a souvenir, but also a kind of mythology." Beyond the physical, however, lie our memories and in them, the pictures stored in our minds' eyes. As writers, aren't these memories—both the physical and the "mementos of the mind"—the essence of our works, the prompts we use to spin the words and phrases into literary tapestries our readers can use to discover something about life, a bit about us, and, in a process, perhaps, a little about themselves?

Many of the photo prompts used here are from the Flash Fiction Challenges managed by the Website *Indies Unlimited*. In a nutshell, the Challenges (which usually begin either every Saturday or Sunday morning at 9 a.m., Pacific time) require participants to write a complete story (plot, characters, hook, and slam-bang finish) in 250 words or fewer. Each must incorporate the elements of a photographic and written prompt. Weekly winners, selected by popular vote, receive the "Flash Fiction Star." Another weekly winner, "Editors' Choice," is selected by the administrators/editors for inclusion in an annual anthology. Announcements of the latter can lag submission by several months.

Theodore Jerome Cohen
Langhorne, Pennsylvania
February 28, 2023

NB: The paperback edition of this book is printed using an updated (November 2022) edition of THE DOVES TYPE® typeface, Robert Green's digital recreation of the Doves Press Fount of Type. See **Endnote 1** for more information on this typeface and its tortured history.

Acknowledgement

I will forever be grateful to my wife, Susan (1943 – 2021)—the love of my life—who provided vital suggestions and, equally important, unswerving support, during the development of most of my writings.

Those we love don't go away,
they walk beside us every day.
Unheard but always near,
still loved, still missed, and very dear.

Martelli, NYPD

A Collection of Excerpts from the
Detective Louis "Lou" Martelli, NYPD,
Mystery/Thriller Series

"Jack is Back" (Photo: K. S. Brooks)
Indies Unlimited, October 27, 2018

Martelli looked to his right, where the visage of a devilish face,
this one celebrating the day when ghosts and witches are said
to appear, seeming smiled at him.

1. Jack is Back

"**W**addaya got for me, Michael?" asked Detective Lou Martelli, NYPD, as he stepped into the garden of a townhouse in the West Village early in the evening on Halloween, 2017.

"The usual," deadpanned Deputy Coroner Michael Antonetti. He pulled a white sheet over the victim, closed his medical bag, stood, and faced the detective. "White male, about 40 years of age, medium build, sliced and diced like that jack-o'-lantern grinnin' at you from over there."

Martelli looked to his right, where the visage of a devilish face, this one celebrating the day when ghosts and witches are said to appear, seeming smiled at him. "Well, he sure looks like he knows something but ain't talkin'," replied Martelli, taking out his notebook. "So, any murder weapon?"

"Oh, yeah, we got a murder weapon, all right," nodded the coroner, handing Martelli a sealed, tagged evidence bag. "Even better than that, we got the whole kit and caboodle; we got ourselves an entire set of murder weapons."

"Whaddaya mean, Michael?"

"What I mean is, we got ourselves a complete set of pumpkin carving sculpting tools. Whoever killed our John Doe, here, musta interrupted the guy while he was working on his pumpkin because the vic's stomach looks like ol' jack's."

"Well, it just confirms what we already know," replied Martelli.

"What's that?"

"Pumpkin carving is one of the most dangerous things a person can do! Don't you remember? There're almost 2000 pumpkin carving injuries nationwide every year during October and November."[1]

---

1 Det. Louis Martelli, NYPD, is the protagonist in six murder mystery/thrillers penned by the author, all of which are based on real life or on stories ripped from the headlines.

"Stakeout" (Photo: endomotion, Big Stock Photo)

This was the third night we had been holed up in the apartment above the used furniture store on Atlantic Avenue in Brooklyn.

---

https://www.amazon.com/gp/product/B07HRFJ8FT/ref=series_rw_dp_sw
Audiobooks also are available for the series on Amazon's *Audible* platform.

2. Stakeout

This was the third night we had been holed up in the apartment above the used furniture store on Atlantic Avenue in Brooklyn. It was 8 p.m. on a chilly November evening. Minutes earlier we had relieved Detectives Eddy Lewis and Mary Fitzpatrick, who had been assigned to cover the previous 12-hour shift. The furniture store had been closed for hours and the street lamps were in full bloom. The NYPD was using this location to stake out what appeared to be an abandoned business establishment. An anonymous tip suggested members of an Iranian foundation linked to the assassination of a Wall Street banker in late October met here.

We were using twin, 35mm digital SLR cameras with ten-megapixel image sensors and manual exposure settings. Both were focused on the entrance to the storefront. The building's windows were covered with butcher paper, but, at the least, we were looking for opportunities to capture images of people entering and leaving the building as well as shots of vehicles of interest.

Despite the fact it was cold outside, we kept the apartment window 'cracked', just to make sure we didn't miss anything happening on the street if, for some reason, both of us happened to be looking away or were otherwise distracted for a moment.

"Tell me again what we know about these people, Lou?" asked Detective Sean O'Keeffe as he checked the cameras for the second time to ensure they were properly aimed and focused.

"It's probably an Iranian front organization," I responded. "The chief said the foundation was registered in the Jebel Ali Free Zone, which is located in the United Arab Emirates. It's only 21 miles southwest of Dubai City and built around Port Rashid, the world's largest man-made port."

"Nice way to hide one's pedigree."

"I'll say. The majority of business in the Free Zone is done by small traders whose names aren't well known. And it doesn't take more than a glance at any map of the area to show you that it's only a hop, skip, and a jump from Port

Rashid to Bandar-e Lengeh, the closest port in Iran. The chief said a person in a high-speed boat could get money and goods that had been shipped to the Jebel Ali Free Zone into Iran in no time. In fact, despite the US embargo on shipments to Iran, trade between the Free Zone and Iran isn't prohibited. There are plenty of companies in the Free Zone that will transship goods to Iran."

"So, this 'Iranian foundation', for all we know, is just a front to move money to Iran in violation of the sanctions we've imposed. Or worse. Hell, they could be funding terrorist organizations directly, for all we know!"

"Bingo! It's not clear how that banker got caught up in the mix, but one thing's for sure: he's dead. One slug through the heart at close range! And the killer's trail leads directly to the shop across the street."

I had no sooner finished speaking when we heard a car door slam. Turning our attention to the window, we observed a lone figure making his way quickly to the building across the street. Sean clicked the shutters of both cameras multiple times, capturing, in rapid succession, sequential images of what appeared to be a man, who, having stepped to the door, first turned to assure himself that no one had seen him, and then, using his key, opened the door and quickly made his way inside.

"What the fu—" I whispered, rubbing my chin.

Sean turned and gave me a quizzical look. "You look like you're seen a ghost? Do you recognize him?"

"Let me see one of those cameras."

He handed me one. I was startled by what I saw in the camera's display screen. Did I know the guy? Hell, I knew him well.

We first met in kindergarten and were inseparable through our senior year of high school. His name was Vince—Vince Ponticelli. Now, he appeared to be about five-ten, 190 pounds, and stout. In high school, however, he was trim and muscular, and sported a full head of pitch-black hear worn in a mullet. A liberal application of Dippity-do was *de rigor* in those days, as was his daily attire consisting of a cotton t-shirt, black jeans, and biker boots.

Even as a kid Vince knew *everything* that went on in Brooklyn, especially if it was the least bit on the shady side. This knowledge, and the people with whom he associated, affected him greatly. It wasn't long before his own life took a turn to the dark side. On the bottom shelf of the bookcase in his bedroom, for example, were four books he had ostensibly used in high school: books on civics, science, algebra, and Spanish. Ponticelli glued them together at the end of our sophomore year, then hollowed out the inside of the stack to form a hiding place for marijuana. His parents never suspected he had the drug, which he sold to friends and acquaintances. I have to admit, too, that in our junior and senior years, he and I used to enjoy a joint now and then, especially after we took our dates home on Saturday night.

"The guy never had a chance," I muttered. "Not that I was a saint. I got into a lot of trouble, most of it with Vince—I mean, you wouldn't believe the things we pulled until my old man, God rest his soul—he was a street cop you know—finally had enough. He grabbed me by the ear after my high school graduation, marched me down to the Army recruiter, and forced me to enlist. I ended up at Fort Rucker in the US Army Aviation Center. You know the rest."

"So, what happened to Vince? Obviously, you haven't been in touch with him."

"Well, I tried talking him into coming into the Army with me, but his parents, with four other mouths to feed, insisted he get a job close to home and start helping out with the family. Vince went down to the docks and found himself a job as a longshoreman. It came with a terrible price, though, because he got involved with the mob.

"On top of that, he got his girlfriend Elena pregnant, which complicated their lives beyond anything you can imagine. Not only did they have to get married, but each of their parents threw them out.

I handed Sean the camera, which he remounted on its tripod and again aimed at the storefront across the street.

"Steph tried to stay in touch with Elena," I continued. "They also were high school classmates. But the tougher things got for her and Vince, the more difficult it was for Steph to learn what was happening.

"Anyway, the last time I heard about Vince was in a letter Steph wrote to me when I was flying Black Hawk combat missions out of Kuwait, something to the effect Elena and Vince's son had died of cancer."

"God, that musta been rough!"

"Ya think? The kid's name was Joey. Elena told Steph he'd been battling leukemia for several years. They thought it was in remission, but then, he died a week short of his tenth birthday. Elena told Steph that watching Joey suffer destroyed Vince. He couldn't take it anymore, she said, and he left them six months before the kid passed."

"Wait! You're telling me the kid's dying, and the guy leaves his wife to deal with it? What the Hell?"

"I know. I couldn't believe it either."

Sean shook his head. "Damn, what goes through some people's minds? How do you leave your wife to deal with something like that?!"

"That's a good question, my friend, a very good question. Let's ask right after we bust him and read 'im his rights."

See Endnote 2.

"Wheel of Fortune" (Photo: Cheshirskiy Kot, Shutterstock)

"I've seen the tattoo of the Wheel of Fortune she has on her back."

3. Wheel of Fortune

"**So,** did you know Katlyn Lundquist well?" asked Special Agent Ron Bishop of the Federal Bureau of Investigation as he took his place next to the sheriff in a front-row pew at Mt. Bethel Church in Columbia, Pennsylvania.

"I guess you could say that," chuckled Police Chief John Packard. "Knew her parents, for sure—Nels and Didrika. Long-time residents of the city. Tragic what happened to them back in '07."

"What happened?" asked Bishop, maintaining his gaze on the other mourners who were filing in to pay their respects before the closed casket, many, apparently, silently beseeching the Lord to protect the soul of the dearly departed before they crossed themselves, turned, and found places to sit in the small country church.

"Died in an automobile accident on the Pennsylvania Turnpike in June of that year," replied Packard. "They'd immigrated to the US in '94 with Katlyn, who was five at the time, best I recall. She was the sole survivor. Nels was the owner of Lundquist Service Corporation, a successful professional laundry and carpet cleaning firm serving the hotel, motel, and bed and breakfast industries in York, Lancaster, and the surrounding areas."

"Wow, that musta been rough on the kid."

"Well, let me tell you, she had it pretty good right up to their deaths. Fact is, the girl was spoiled rotten. They never disciplined her. Which pretty much explains why she was such a hellion. And the older she got, the worse it became."

"So, she had a few run-ins with the law?"

"A few?! That, my friend, is an understatement. I first ran into her right after she entered high school. I won't bore you with all the details, Ron, but in her junior year alone I recall charging her with trespass and disorderly conduct, possession of a controlled substance, possession of drug paraphernalia, and public drunkenness."

"Man, you really had your hands full just with her."

11

"I'll say, Now, mind you, her parents always took care of those problems, which is to say they made them go away."

"What you mean to say, John, is they paid the fines or bought off the parties harmed."

"Well, when they could. When they couldn't, our juvenile court stepped in, so there were some actions taken there. But you couldn't access the records, Ron, because as you know, she being a minor and all, any court proceedings would have been sealed.

"After her parents were killed, she seemed to straighten out for the most part, and we didn't have any major problems with her. But she continued to use fake IDs now and then, usually when she was carded at one of the local roadhouses. The bartenders all knew her, and it became something of a joke with them."

"So, when did she start to go by the name Nicole Davis?"

"I never was sure, Ron."

"Well, that's the name we knew her by in New York City."

"It must've had some special meaning to her. Best I could tell, it's a name Lundquist used since she was a freshman in high school. She had fake IDs made using that name so she could buy alcohol and cigarettes for herself and her friends. When she started driving, she carried several driver's licenses ostensibly issued by different states. She used those whenever she was carded. All of them were fabricated using her picture and the name Nicole Davis."

"So, how do you suppose she came to end up in the New York City area, John?"

"Well, as you know, a little over two years ago, we started having trouble with the mob moving into Lancaster and York. A cartage association run by the Mafia was attempting to take over the garbage, trash, and recycling business in those towns. Basically, the mob established their own trash companies in those cities and then, by talking to the customers of established independent operators, convinced them to shift their business to the mob by undercutting their current trash haulers' prices. One independent operator who fought them was Ryan Belmont. He operated a trash and recycling business in Lancaster with his son, Sanford. They both were found shot to death in June 2012. The killer or killers were never found, but it was always assumed the mob was responsible."

"Okay, I understand. But how does Katlyn Lundquist play into that?"

"Well, sir, I heard—and mind you, this is unsubstantiated—she was seen with Jimmie Lupinacci's son, Tommie, a real psychopath if there ever was one, at a nightclub in Pittsburgh on two successive weekends in early September 2012."

"That would be Jimmie Lupinacci, the mobster."

"One and the same."

"And once you've seen Lundquist, you'd never forget her. She was exquisite. Blonde, svelte, with sculpted facial features, she was a Swedish beauty.

"Oh, yes, I know."

"Apparently, Jimmie couldn't take his eyes—or his hands—off of her. It didn't take long for word of those sightings to get back to us."

"So, you're thinking was that Tommie Lupinacci was behind the Belmont murders."

"No question in my mind, Ron."

"Well, sir, at about the same time all of this was happening, Lundquist suddenly puts her family's home up for sale. She never had to worry about money, so when an offer came in, albeit lowballed according to her agent, she accepted. Then, she sold her car the next day, gave her real estate agent power of attorney, and disappeared.

"Except that's, apparently, where you picked up on her, Ron, if I understand correctly."

"That's right. We'd been watching the Lupinacci's attempts to move into on southeastern Pennsylvania for some time and saw Tommie's new girlfriend as someone we might be able to 'flip' for information. We knew her as Nicole Davis, of course, and easily determined he had put her up in nice apartment on Henry Street in Brooklyn. Given the circumstances, it didn't take too much pressure to convince Davis—that is, Lundquist—to work with us. Basically, we threatened to charge her with conspiracy and other assorted crimes and misdemeanors.

"In the end, she went along with our plan to wire her apartment, tap her phone, and the like, for the purpose of gathering the evidence we needed to take down the Lupinacci family. Secret liaison meetings between Lundquist and one of our agents took place, as needed, in the woman's room in a small diner around the corner from the local tattoo parlor she frequented. As you know, she was into body art."

"I'll say. I've seen the tattoo of the Wheel of Fortune she has on her back. It's the same symbol found on tarot cards. But that wasn't all. The New York City deputy coroner also photographed tats on her back and upper right arm. The lady was a real showcase, that's for sure."

"So, how did she end up murdered?"

"It's clear Lupinacci—who was married, by the way—went to Lundquist's apartment to drink and have sex out of sight of prying eyes. She liquored him up every time he was there, something I encouraged her to do. Hell, he probably even paid for the booze. And given Lupinacci's volatile nature, it wouldn't surprise me if he picked up her phone after having one too many and made calls to North Carolina and Pennsylvania on occasion without even thinking about the consequences. It's only after he sobered up the next morning that he might have had second thoughts about having made those calls—*if he even remembered making them.* It probably wasn't until bad things started to happen—as in the case of several truckloads of his cigarettes being seized—that the connection occurred to him."

"So, he put two and two together—"

"And had her killed," said the sheriff, completing the agent's sentence.

"Yes, we found her dumped in Thomas Paine Park, within spitting distance of 26 Federal Plaza, well after midnight one night. No identification on the body. Her clothes, which could have been purchased at any of a hundred stores in the five boroughs, weren't disturbed, and a preliminary examination showed she wasn't sexually assaulted. One shot in the back of the head. Classic sign of a mob hit."

"Well, I hope she didn't suffer."

"There were no signs of a struggle, John. The autopsy suggested she knew her—"

"Why, hello, Father. Ron, allow me to introduce Father Glenn Everett. He's been watching over our flock for the past 20 years. Father, this is Ron Bishop. He's with the FBI."

The two men rose to greet the pastor. The men shook hands.

"Agent Bishop," intoned Father Everett, "I understand we have you to thank for returning Katlyn to us."

"Well, Father, it was the least I could do, given I feel responsible for her death."

"How's that, Agent Bishop?"

"Well, I keep going over and over in my mind the things we asked Ms. Lindquist to do for the Bureau. On hindsight, I wonder if we didn't push her too far, too fast. But then, there were urgent matters to address regarding the cases we were working on, the deaths that already had occurred in a number of those cases, including some in Lancaster and York, and— Well, I constantly find myself asking the Lord for forgiveness. Butt never seems to be enough," said the agent, shaking his head. "Even now, I wake up, night after night—"

"Agent Bishop—may I call you Ron?"

"Yes, of course."

"Ron, you must always remember the words of Isaiah, Chapter 65, Verse 24: *And it shall come to pass, that before they call, I will answer; and while they are yet speaking, I will hear.* You must take comfort in the thought the Lord already knows what is in your heart."

"Thank you, Father. I needed to hear that," said Ron, tears forming in his eyes.

The sheriff and the agent sat as Father Everett turned, walked to the altar, and with the crowd hushed, began the funeral service.

Preceding Lundquist's interment. Agent Ron Bishop spoke eloquently of Katlyn's spirit and zest for life. "It is because of her dedication to seeing justice done, to ensuring the murderers of many in your area stand trial, that I stand before you today to sing her praises," said Bishop, holding the lectern with both hands to steady himself. "To her, the path she took was not one of choice but of necessity. And for that she paid the ultimate price. Certainly, she will be remembered all the days of our lives as someone truly special. And so, I say to her, rest in peace, dear Katlyn. And may the Lord bless and keep you, forever and ever."

See Endnote 3.

"Accidentally, On Purpose, Dead" (Photo: OdessaA_L, Big Stock Photo)

The last thing he ever would see was the split trunk of an old oak tree coming toward him at a speed of 62 miles

4. Accidentally, On Purpose, Dead

Conference Room 807 in building at 26 Federal Plaza, home to the FBI's New York City field office, was something like a small college lecture hall, with its stage, podium, and drop-down screen for visual presentations. A projection system hung from the ceiling. Seats toward the rear of the room were elevated, as was the stage. To the left of the stage was a credenza; there, the Bureau had provided donuts and pastries together with regular and decaf coffee, a selection of teas, hot water, cups and spoons, cream, sweetener, and cocktail napkins.

I'm Lou Martelli, a New York Police Department detective. My partner is Sean O'Keefe. We were here for a presentation by the Bureau on Operation Eagle Justice. It was a combined FBI-NYPD sting operation intended to take down an effort by the Mafia to establish itself in the small Pennsylvania town of Lancaster.

As we entered the room, Special Agent William "Bill" Landau of the FBI moved to the podium and clipped a small microphone to his shirt. Flipping a switch, he began counting: "One, two, three; hello radio. Does that sound okay?"

Everyone nodded, with one or two in the room shouting "Yes, sir."

"Okay, ladies and gents, let's get started."

O'Keeffe and I hurriedly grabbed cups of coffee and several small pastries while others raced for refills and sweets before taking seats.

The first PowerPoint slide, containing yellow lettering on a blue background, was already on the screen. Emblazoned on it was the name of the operation and the cartoon of an eagle alighting with talons extended, its prey, a small rodent, seconds away from capture: Operation Eagle Justice.

Landau moved to the next slide. "Jimmie Lupinacci, head of the Lupinacci 'family' and one of the biggest players in the New York City Mafia. He's one helluva businessman, I'll give him that. And while he's gradually moved into more legitimate businesses of late, he still has his hand in the pocket of every company that moves freight in to and out of every major New York and New Jersey port and airport. He also controls several companies that service the docks and airports, insure cargo, and so forth. You get the picture. He's a ruthless son-of-a-bitch, and we're watching him and his people closely."

He switched to the next slide.

"Now, here's the object of our affection: Tommie Lupinacci, Jimmie's only son. He was knighted King of Trash by his father in 2005, responsible for overseeing the mob's New York City cartage association, though he also dabbles in cigarette smuggling from time to time. This guy's even more dangerous than his father. Tommie's a certified, one-hundred-percent psychopath, someone who would as soon shoot you as look at you. We suspect he was responsible for giving the order to kill our informant Nicole Davis, aka Katlyn Lundquist, here in New York City, something NYPD Martelli and O'Keeffe, who you'll meet in a few minutes, very smartly kept out of the public eye for us until we were able to contact them.

"Not content with running the mob's trash and recycling business in the five boroughs and northern New Jersey, Tommie spread his wings into Pennsylvania some years ago, where, by word or by force, he started to push the small independent operators out of business. In at least one case, that of Ryan Belmont and his son, Lou, we believe he had them killed when they wouldn't shut down their trash and recycling operation. So far, local authorities haven't been able to come up with sufficient evidence to charge Tommie or anyone associated with him with the murders. That's something we hope to rectify with this operation, though it's only part of our focus."

From there, Landau went on to review the next layer of details regarding the Lupinacci crime family and what the Bureau knew about its members and operations. When he finished, he introduced the other members of the Bureau's team who would be working with Sean and me in Lancaster. First up to bat was Special Agent Amanda Whitman. "I'll manage the office for the little business we formed there. It's called US Trash and Recycling."

"Nothing like being in their face with that name," Sean quipped.

"Well, we're not exactly hiding under a bushel basket," Amanda shot back, laughing.

Landau then introduced Special Agent Stan Easton. "I'm an accountant. I'll be driving down to Lancaster with you Saturday morning to relieve the agent who's been working in my position for the last six months. Amanda will be driving us."

Easton, an older man, lived with his wife of 20 years in one of many new high-rise buildings springing up from the landscape in the Bronx. As I would learn on the trip to Pennsylvania, they lived alone, having lost a daughter at the age of ten to a degenerative lung condition. Now, they both spent what money and time they could spare supporting the Make-a-Wish Foundation. A twenty-five-year veteran of the Bureau, Easton specialized in accounting, sometimes working as a forensic accountant. But he was a fully qualified FBI agent and had been on many a difficult assignment that required him to use his firearm on occasion.

Anyway, the Bureau had done its homework. Before we had even left New York City, they already had set all of us up with fake identities, created bogus files on us in the Pennsylvania state motor vehicle department's database, provided extra cash for us to throw around, as necessary, and gave us a company credit card for gas. The cell phones we were given were to be changed weekly. They were untraceable. We could use them to call our families but our families were *not* to call us. If there was an emergency at home, families were to call the Bureau, and *its* personnel would provide assistance.

And, if we got into trouble, say, with "The Law," we were to call Amanda. She was prepared to come in and get us out of town, even if she had to take us out in chains on trumped-up federal charges. The important thing was *not* to compromise the operation under any circumstances!

Once in Lancaster, we set about on a plan to make things as uncomfortable as possible for Tommie Lupinacci and his fellow mobsters. For example, on a typical morning, Amanda would hand us a map, say, of North Lancaster, and ask us to follow one of Lupinacci's trash trucks as its crew made their morning rounds. "They'll start around 7am. The customers are mostly 'mom and pop' shops. Stay a good block or so behind them. Watch where they pick up the trash. Then, later, go in, drop off a brochure, and if possible, talk to the owner about switching to us. Offer a 50-percent discount with a one-year price guarantee. Don't be surprised if you don't get any takers. There's a lot of fear in the business community. Frankly, I don't care if we get their business or not. What I want is to be a thorn in Lupinacci's side. I want to goad him into doing something stupid, something we can use to take down his entire operation.

And, if you run into some guy named Tiny and his sidekick, back off. I don't need more any of my agents ending up in the ER."

Ah, yes, the gruesome, twosome: Matt "Tiny" Farmer, and his sidekick, a little prick by the name of Larry Halstead. We had learned some months earlier, before Sean and I arrived in Lancaster, they had boxed Special Agents Al Knots and Burt Linden in with their cars, with Farmer—all 6-feet and 300 pounds of him—in front and Halstead in back. On that occasion, Tiny got out, came back to the agents' car, and told Al to get out. But Al wouldn't move. So, Tiny grabbed the left rear-view mirror and ripped it off the car. That pissed Al off, so ever so slowly, he released the latch, and when Tiny least expected it, he pushed the door open with both hands, smashing it into Tiny's left knee. Tiny went down for the count as Al stepped outside, but as Tiny was getting on his feet, he sucker punched Al in the face with his right fist.

"Wow," said O'Keeffe when he heard the story, "that musta hurt."

"I've had better days, Sean. Anyway, by that time you could hear a siren—somebody must've called the cops—so Tiny and Halstead beat it out of there. The patrolman asks if there's a problem, and I tell him, 'No, just a little disagreement.' He knows who we are—that is, by our fake names—and who we work for, so he has a pretty good idea who was behind my injuries."

Here, Linden picked up the story. "But he didn't see what had happened, and because we didn't appear to want to do anything, he just told us to be careful and drove off. At that point, I took Al to the ER and got him stitched up. Told the attending physician he had run into a door. Thank God US Trash has good health insurance."

At the time, we laughed. "Well, look on the bright side, guys," said Amanda. "I'm sure word was passed to Lupinacci that we were on the prowl again to take customers away from him. Remember, that's what got the Belmonts killed. But it's got to piss off Tommie Lupinacci because it interferes with his plans to expand into Pennsylvania."

Special Agent Landau's words rang in Martelli's ears: *I want to goad him into doing something stupid, something we can use to take down his entire operation.*

Agent Stan Easton had not intended to stay at the office late. His work on US Trash and Recycling's ledgers had been finished that afternoon. Even after he had straightened up his workplace, there should have been sufficient time to return to his motel in daylight. But it had been ten days since he spoke with his wife Jean in the Bronx, and tonight, the news he received about her father through the Bureau was not good. So, they spoke at great length.

"I had to call hospice for him today, Stan," said his wife, her voice trembling. "He was complaining of terrible pain to the nursing home staff, and nothing they did helped. His doctor finally arrived and gave him some relief. But I don't think he has much longer to live. Do you think you can come home? I need you. We need you."

"I'll check with my boss, honey. I'm sure we can work something out. I'm so sorry it's come to this for your dad. He's always been so strong and energetic. I still can't believe what's happened to him."

"I know. If only they had been able to administer that new treatment for prostate cancer back in 2007 that he was counting on, the one the FDA initially turned down. Remember?"

"I remember, the one developed by that little company in Seattle."

"Yes. And I'm still angry at the Federal government for not opening an investigation into the corruption surrounding the whole matter. Lots of people at the FDA and on Wall Street have blood on their hands, that's for sure."[2] The bitterness in her voice was palpable.

"And then, in 2010, when the treatment finally was approved, remember how Dad no longer qualified for it and how we had to use radiation and those other horrible drugs that totally destroyed his quality of life?" She broke down and sobbed.

Easton talked with his wife for the better part of an hour, attempting to reassure her that she had done the right thing by bringing hospice in, that her father was in good hands, that hospice would ensure he was not in pain, that her father and she already had put his affairs in order . . . and that, in short, anything and everything that could have been done for him had been done.

---

2 Mitchell, Mark, *The Dendreon Effect: How Felons, Con-Men and Wall Street Insiders Manipulate High-Tech Stocks*, Silver Lake Publishing, December 30, 2011. eBook, Amazon ASIN: B006RXHSA4

But still, the facts were, she was alone and needed him to be with her. Of that he was all too aware. Unfortunately, he could not simply pick up and leave without first talking to Special Agent Whitman, who, in turn, would have to talk with Bishop. But this was not something he could discuss with his wife. She had no idea where Bishop was, much less what he was doing.

"Look, honey, my boss gets in early, usually around 6 a.m. I'll talk with her first thing tomorrow. If all goes well, I could be home by noon. The work I'm doing is important, but I think I know someone who could jump in and take over immediately."

His wife sounded reassured. They said their goodbyes on a positive note.

Easton ended the call with his wife, put his cell phone into his pocket, turned off the office lights, armed the security system, stepped outside, and locked the building's door. He appeared deep in thought as he plodded towards his car, no doubt preoccupied by the disturbing call he had had with his wife.

It was well past the time Easton normally ate dinner. Still, a man had to eat, and there were several diners from which to choose. One in particular, north of Ironville, served a great meal at a special price on Wednesdays.

Concentrating on his driving, and with his mind apparently distracted by thoughts of his wife, Easton was unaware of a car that had been following him since he turned right off westbound Route 462 heading north on Prospect Road toward the diner. As time went by, the car came closer and closer to him, though it never appeared threatening.

Easton finally became aware of the other vehicle as he approached the site of an FM radio broadcast tower. There, the other vehicle's headlights momentarily produced a blinding glare in his left rear-view mirror as Easton negotiated a sharp left curve. Easton took notice but appeared to dismiss the annoyance. *It's still relatively early, and heavier-than-usual traffic is to be expected,* he thought.

Seconds after Easton passed the radio station's tower, the car trailing him sped up, closing the distance between the two vehicles to less than ten feet.

The agent looked into his rear-view mirror, surprised at the aggressiveness of the other driver. But before he could comprehend what might be happening, the second car rammed the rear bumper of Easton's rental car before immediately backing off.

Easton frantically fought to retain control of his vehicle. Then, the pursuing car rammed him again, this time maintaining contact as the other driver gunned his engine, pushing Easton's car off the road and into the trees on the last turn before the road straightened for the run into Ironville.

The last thing FBI Agent Stan Easton of the Bronx, New York City, ever would see was the split trunk of an old oak tree coming toward him at a speed of 62 miles per hour.

See Endnote 4.

"506" (Photo: (K. S. Brooks)
Indies Unlimited, May 29, 2021[3]

"If it's any help, the address we had on file for Celestia's family is 506 McClellan Lane, here in Syracuse."

---

3 Though the photo prompt is from Indies Unlimited's weekly competition for May 29, 2021, the story was too long to submit for competition. That said, I thank Ms. Brooks for inspiring me to write this tale.

5. 506

"**D**oes the name Tia or Celestia ring a bell?" asked NYPD Homicide Detective Lou Martelli. He was on his cell phone talking to Edward Lane, Principal, Marquis de Lafayette High School.

"Oh, yes, of course," replied Lane. "Very bright young lady. Attractive, too. As I recall, she was here under a scholarship provided by an anonymous benefactor. Unfortunately, Tia left in the middle of her junior year. I must say, it was quite unexpected."

"How so?"

"Well, one day, her father just walked into my office and abruptly pulled her out of school . . . said something about his being transferred out-of-country. The family was gone two days later, lock, stock, and barrel. No one ever saw them again. Nor did anyone ever learn what happened to her or her family. They simply vanished into thin air."

"Who did the father work for?"

"I haven't a clue . . . and before you ask, no, our records wouldn't show that kind of information. Yes, they would show a student's emergency contact names, address, and telephone numbers, but in most cases, these would almost always be their parent's names and home telephone or cell phone numbers."

Lane paused while he consulted his computer files. "If it's any help, the address we had on file for Celestia's family is 506 McClellan Lane, here in Syracuse.

"I recall her mother was a stay-at-home mom because there were two much younger children in the family. We talked about them briefly on one parent-teacher's night at the high school."

Martelli thought for a moment. "Ed, when I was in high school, we had a photography club. Do you have one?"

"You bet, one of the best in the area."

"So, there were always lots of guys and gals taking photographs of just about anything and everything throughout the school year, and maybe into the summer?"

"Absolutely. In fact, we used to do most of our own film developing and printing using the old dark room in the basement of the administration building. Posted many of the club's photos on the bulletin boards throughout the school. Still do, in fact, though today everything is digital. We also use these photos in the school newspaper, for event publicity offsite—for example, on the bulletin boards at the local grocery and drug stores—and in our yearbooks."

"So, it's safe to assume Tia appears in some of these photos, whether on purpose or by accident."

"I would think so, Detective."

"Ed, this is very important. You may be one of the few people who not only remember Tia, but also, who remember what she looks like.

"I know this may be an imposition, but could I ask you, for starters, to go through the school newspapers and photos for the years in which Tia was a student. If you find any pictures of her, any pictures at all, regardless of their size and quality, please make copies using your cell phone and e-mail them to me. It's vital we find this woman.

"I wish I could tell you more. Perhaps someday I'll be in a position to do that. But for now, trust me when I tell you she may hold the key to our understanding of what happened to her classmates, Trent Morrison and Brent Hallaway."

Lane didn't immediately respond. In fact, for a moment, Martelli thought he had lost the connection.

"Ed? Ed? Are you still there?"

"Yes, I'm still here, Detective. I don't know if I can do what you ask. Don't you need some kind of warrant to obtain those pictures? I mean, first of all, the pictures are of minors. And second, the photos are the property of a private institution—this high school."

"I understand your concerns, Ed. But as you said, many of the pictures are already in the public domain, so to speak, by having been published in the school newspaper, which certainly must have been taken outside the school, or by having been posted in stores around the local neighborhood.

"Now, we could get a judge to issue a warrant, if that's required. But frankly, if the press got wind of that, think what might happen when they start poking around. You certainly don't need the publicity, let alone the interruptions. And believe me, the press can be relentless . . . and ruthless. If there's even the whiff—"

"I get it, Detective. I'll do as you ask and be in contact as soon as I have something."

"And Ed—"

"Yes?"

"I don't have to tell you how sensitive this is. So, please keep this just between us."

"I understand. You can count on me. I'll start looking through the school's newspapers and other photos as soon as we hang up."

Martelli's partner, Detective-Specialist Sean O'Keeffe, sat silently through the entire exchange between Martelli and Ed Lane. He could hear both sides of the conversation. When his partner finally ended the call and put his cell phone on the seat next to him, O'Keeffe turned to him and chuckled. "I got news for you, Buddy. You don't stand a snowball's chance in Hell of finding that woman. I don't care if Ed gives you a thousand pictures of her—they could even have been taken yesterday—she'll never be found."

"What the hell are you talking about, Sean?"

"She's in the witness protection program, Lou."

See Endnote 5.

"Porch" (Photo: K.S. Brooks)
Indies Unlimited, June 19, 2021[4]

**She stepped back, motioning them to step into the screened porch
that encircled the lower level of the house on three sides.**

---

4 Though the photo prompt is from Indies Unlimited's weekly competition
for June 19, 2021, the story was too long to submit for competition. That said,
I thank Ms. Brooks for inspiring me to write this tale.

6. Porch

"Well, that went well," said NYPD Homicide Detective Louis "Lou" Martelli as he and Sheriff Geoffrey Ward walked across the grass in the front of Weston's home on their way to Mrs. Diane Goodman's cottage on Lake George.

The sheriff laughed. "Thank God we caught Weston's other neighbor, Arnold Braun, on a good day, Lou."

Braun, a recluse, lived in a small two-story cottage set back some 75 feet from the lake. Neither a 'busybody' nor a gossip, he had few friends despite the fact he had lived in the community more than 20 years. He rarely ventured out, and when he did, it was only to shop for food or conduct business at the bank in town. He was a hoarder; his front room was stacked floor to ceiling with books, magazines, and newspapers, with only a small pathway available to walk from the front door to the back of the house. To say he didn't want to get involved in the men's murder investigation was an understatement.

"Yeah, well, lots of luck getting *his* fingerprints. I suspect you'll have to hogtie the gentleman and haul him into town before that's done."

"Aw, he'll settle down. I'll bring some schnapps with me tomorrow, and we'll finish up before he has no more than two shots."

Deputy Sheriff Johnson and NYPD Homicide Sean O'Keeffe, sitting in the deputy's patrol car, appeared to be engaged in an animated conversation involving the shooting of rifles at targets located well above their heads. "My guess is war stories," the sheriff said, laconically. "Johnson was in the 10th Mountain Division . . . Nuristan Province, Iraq, I believe."

Martelli chuckled. "O'Keeffe was over there, as well. I'm sure they'll have more than enough stories to tell each other. Some may even be true."

The men continued walking to Goodman's cottage, a traditional two-story lake home that sat 100 feet back from the water. They had barely finished climbing the front steps when the door opened."

"Well, if it isn't Sheriff Ward. How are you, Geoff?"

"Just fine, Diane. Thanks for asking. This here is Detective Louis Martelli of the New York Police Department. We were wondered if you might have a little time to answer a few questions regarding Phil Weston."

She smiled broadly. "Of course, of course. Please come in. It's so nice to have company."

Goodman, a widow, was in her mid-70s. Short, with gray hair, she was more than a few pounds overweight. "I'm big boned," is what she told her closest friends when they would discuss their weight problems while playing Mah-jongg on Wednesday afternoons. Goodman was dressed in a bright rainbow-striped housecoat and smelled as if she had just taken a scented bath.

She stepped back, motioning them to step into the screened porch that encircled the lower level of the house on three sides. On the left, in the far corner of the porch, the men could see a dining area. A couch was positioned to the right of the dining table, the first of several pieces of furniture that Goodman and her guests used when they read or simply relaxed while enjoying a refreshing lake breeze.

During the winter, storm windows replaced the screens that had been hung over the windows for the summer. As well, the dark green canvas awnings on the lake side of the house had been rolled up to let the sun and lake breezes in. The awnings would be dropped in early November to protect the house from winter's onslaught.

To the right of the porch's front door was a door that led to the cottage's kitchen while in front of them, another door led to the living room.

"Gentlemen . . . please . . . go into the living room. I'll join you in a minute. How do you take your coffee?"

"I'll take mine with milk, Diane."

"Fine, Geoff. And you, Detective?"

"Please call me Lou, Diane. I take mine black . . . straight up."

"Okay, Lou. I'll be back in a minute. Please, make yourselves at home."

Martelli looked around. The living room was an anachronism. The year may have been 2011 but the room was painted and decorated as if it were as early as the mid-1930s but certainly not much later than the outbreak of World War II. The walls and ceiling were painted light beige while large, thick, Persian carpets covered the hardwood floor. A darkly stained upright piano stood next to the stairs leading to the second floor, which housed three small bedrooms and a bathroom. Opulent chairs, carefully positioned around a coffee table in the center of the living room, were covered in vintage brocade fabrics while several display cabinets filled with family pictures and porcelain artifacts lined two windowless walls. Appropriately placed end tables covered with knick-knacks and tchotchkes rounded out the room's furnishings.

Wow, thought Martelli, *for all intents and purposes, time has stood still. This room hasn't changed in 75 years.*

"Here you are, gentleman. Geoff, I'll let you pour your own milk. And I brought something for us to nosh on while we talk. Just don't tell Dr. Allerton I ate any of these."

She set a plate of homemade cinnamon rolls on the coffee table. "She's been warning me about my blood sugar level, so I'm trying to cut back on my sweets. But I still cheat a little, now and then." She put the forefinger of her right hand over her lips.

Martelli picked right up on what she was saying. "Your secret is safe with me, Diane."

She giggled.

"This really is a beautiful home you have," he continued, attempting to break the ice.

"It was given to my father by his uncle in the early 1950s. They worked together during World War II. When the uncle retired to Florida, he gave my father this home in exchange for one dollar. We used it as a summer home until my father died in 1967, and then, my mother and I lived in it until she died in 2005. Now I have it. It's just like it always was. Nothing's changed."

Martelli smiled. "I imagine that's a great comfort to you."

"Not everything has to change, Lou. It's possible to find happiness even in the simplest of things . . . a cool lake breeze, fireflies on a hot summer night, a spring thunderstorm. They are as enjoyable and comforting to me now as they were in 1953."

She smiled, closed her eyes momentarily, and nodded. Then she turned and stared out through the room's large picture window, across the porch toward the gazebo in the back yard, and beyond to the lake, as if in her mind's eye she still could see her family as they were when she was a little girl. Slowly she turned back to look at the men.

"Well, Detective, you didn't come all this way to hear me talk about this house and my family. How can I help you?"

"Diane, I can't go into too much detail because of the nature of my investigation, but I will tell you that Mr. Weston did not die of natural causes."

Goodman stopped chewing her food and stared at Martelli. "What?"

"I know this will come as a shock. We don't know who killed him. Nor do we have a motive."

Goodman swallowed and then sat silently, attempting to make sense of something that clearly made no sense to her. Slowly, she wiped her mouth with a linen napkin.

"I can't believe it."

The men let what Martelli had just told her sink in.

Finally, the sheriff spoke. "Diane, if there's anything you can remember about Phil regarding the last few days before his death, it could be of immense importance to our investigation."

"Well, let me think. Phil and I never spoke, of course. Never had any reason to. Years ago, he made it crystal clear that he wasn't interested in establishing any kind of neighborly relationship with me. Every once in a while, I'd see him talking to Arnold Braun—he's another strange one, that Braun fellow—but even those exchanges appeared to have petered out a while back."

Sheriff Ward picked up the conversation. "Did Phil have any visitors over the years that you recall, Diane?"

"Let's see. Oh, yes, several years ago there was a couple and their daughter who came to visit him in the summer. If I remember correctly, they were here two or three times . . . always in the middle of July. But they didn't show up last year. Nor did I see the family this year."

"Are you sure about that, Diane?"

"Oh, yes. Other than that couple and their child, no one ever came to see Phil. Their visits aren't something I would forget."

"Do you remember anything about them? For example, what did they look like? What kind of car did they drive? Anything at all?"

"Well, they weren't Caucasians, if that's what you mean."

"How so?" asked Martelli.

"Their skin seemed darker. And their features were different. They could have been Middle Eastern."

"And their car? Do you know the make?"

"What do I know? My father always drove a Packard *Clipper* . . . the last one was turquoise and white with big whitewall tires. Now, *that* was a real car, not like the junk they sell today."

Martelli laughed. "I take that as a 'no.'"

Goodman laughed. "Your mother didn't raise no dumb kid, Lou. But I can tell you this. The man showed up over there—alone—the day before Phil was found dead, and he wasn't driving the same car he drove when his family—at least I think it was his family—came to Phil's on earlier visits. The car he drove this time was small and gray; when he came with his family, he drove a larger car . . . one of those, what do they call them? Oh, yes . . . SUVs. And that one was white."

Martelli was busy taking notes as Sheriff Ward asked the next question. "How long did he stay this time?"

"Oh, maybe 20 minutes, 25 minutes, tops. Which surprised me, because before, when the three of them came to visit, they always stayed a couple of hours. Anyway, I was puttering around the porch when I saw him pull Phil's front door shut. Then, he turned and walked to his car—"

"Did he appear to be in a hurry?"

"Not particularly. He threw his briefcase in the back seat, got in the driver's seat, started the engine, and drove away. I didn't think anything of it."

Martelli thought for a minute. "If I brought an artist up here, Diane, is it possible the two of you might be able to come up with a sketch of the man?"

"I doubt it, Lou. Not that I wouldn't be willing to give it a try, but I only saw the side of the man's head, and from quite a distance at that."

"Okay, I understand. Just one or two more questions, then. Could you venture a guess as to the age of the people in the family? We understand there also was a child . . . a girl."

"Well, when I last saw the woman, which was two years ago, I'd say she was in her early 30s. The little girl could not have been more than 4 years old at the time. I don't know . . . she looked very young and frail."

"And the man?"

"I'd say he was in his mid- to late 30s."

The men finished their cinnamon rolls and coffee, wiped their mouths, and stood up.

Goodman looked up at them. "Anything else I can do for you, gentlemen?"

"Well," said Martelli, "I sure could use a bathroom."

"I'll second that," said the sheriff."

"It's at the top of the stairs, on your right. But don't flush the toilet until you've both used it! I'm on a well here. If you both flush, you'll stir up the sand at the bottom of the well, and then, I'll have problems with my pump!"

See Endnote 6.

"Missing" (Photo: K. S. Brooks)
Indies Unlimited, June 26, 2021[5]

**"Whaddaya got for me, Tony?" yelled
NYPD Homicide Detective Louis "Lou" Martelli**

---

5 Though the photo prompt is from Indies Unlimited's weekly competition for June 26, 2021, the story was too long to submit for competition. That said, I thank Ms. Brooks for inspiring me to write this tale.

7. Missing

"Whaddaya got for me, Tony?" yelled NYPD Homicide Detective Louis "Lou" Martelli as he and his partner, Detective Sean O'Keeffe, made their way slowly over the dirty coastal industrial lot to where the search and rescue dog handler and his canine partner were working."

"Nothin', Lou; a whole lot of nothin," the handler called back over his shoulder.

"Just like the TV insurance commercial says, Lou," his partner deadpanned. "You get a whole lot of nothin' with Tony Paglione and his dog, Luca."

"That's good, Sean, really good. Did you make that up all yourself, or did you need help?" snapped Tony, somewhat annoyed.

Sgt. Tony Paglione and his dog, Luka, had been searching the area for nearly two hours before the detectives arrived. The temperature now was in the mid-80s, and neither he nor his dog were comfortable working under these conditions.

"Look, guys, I've been over this entire area three times since 8 o'clock this morning—*this entire* area. Luka alerted every time on this particular patch next to the road. It's clear the area was dug up recently—at the least, the ground was disturbed. I did some poking around; you know, removed a little sand and dirt here and there near the surface, but each time, Luka lost interest. If a body were here, he would have sat and stayed. Whoever *was* buried here—assuming someone was—has recently been moved."

"So, as far as you can say, this probably is just another dry hole when it comes to this investigation. Too bad, it took us more than a week of 'round-the-clock investigations just to identify this place as a potential gravesite," lamented Lou.

"Well, it's not a complete bust, Lou."

Martelli's and O'Keeffe's eyebrows went up. "Whaddaya talkin' about, Tony? Spit it out!" cried Sean, eager for a lead, any lead, in the possible

37

homicide of a famous heiress who disappeared without a trace more than a week earlier after a rumored affair with a mobster.

"Well, I always park well outside a search area, never knowing what's going to be found. So, when we arrived this morning, I parked on the asphalt road adjacent to the beach and headed in at the edge of the unpaved road. That's when I noticed tire tracks on the road itself. It must've sprinkled or misted during the night, making it easy to see the tread marks. They had to be recent, so I snapped a few shots and sent them to Forensics."

"And?!" asked Lou, impatiently.

"And, Forensics said they were made by a Michelin tire. In fact, they said the tires were Primacy MXM4 Touring Radial Tires, which, because of their price—over $500 apiece—are not all that common among SUV owners. It shouldn't be difficult to get a list of who may recently have purchased some or, after checking with dealers, who had vehicles delivered with these tires as original equipment."

"Booyah!" yelled Martelli," pumping his right fist up and down in the air. "I don't care what they say about you and Luca, Tony. You guys are all right!"

See Endnote 7.

"Magic" (Photo: K.S. Brooks)
Indies Unlimited, August 7, 2021[6]

**"It was magic. We danced on the terrace and
watched the Moon set over the lake."**

---

6 Though the photo prompt is from Indies Unlimited's weekly competition
for August 7, 2021, the story below was too long to submit for competition.
That said, a shorter version, to be found in **Endnote 8**, *was* submitted. The
shorter version won the weekly competition.

8. Magic

Homicide detective Louis "Lou" Martelli, NYPD, threw his suitcase on the bed, headed for the bathroom, shaved, and then, splashed aftershave on his face. After drying it with a face towel, he sat on one of the twin beds in his motel room and dialed his house on his cell phone. It took only two rings before he heard his wife's voice.

"Ah, the Italian Stallion," answered Stephanie, his wife and high school sweetheart, "galloping through the New York countryside, igniting lust in the hearts of young maidens and envy in the minds of their boyfriends."

"I'm not so sure about that galloping part . . . maybe a little cantering, perhaps, and a trot now and then."

She laughed. Their relationship was as fresh and youthful as the day they met.

"Well, you still seem able to get out on the dance floor at the precinct's Christmas Party and put the younger officers to shame."

"Speaking of dancing," he said, "you'll never guess who has a dinner date tonight, followed by a night of dancing at a local night club."

"Sean? You're kidding!"

"Just like you women. You can't stand to see a handsome, single, happy-go-lucky guy enjoying life to the fullest. As far as you're concerned, a man isn't fulfilled unless he's married and tied down with ten children."

"Keep it up, Detective-Investigator Louis Martelli, Master of All He Surveys, and your sex life going forward will give new meaning to the word 'celibate!'"

"Ha! We'll see who caves first!"

They laughed as if they were teasing each other before classes began during their high school years.

Truth be told, Stephanie Martelli would have loved to see her husband's partner, Sean O'Keeffe, find a lovely woman and settle down, but for now, that didn't seem to be in the cards. True, Sean never was at a loss for finding beautiful women to date, and he always showed up at the precinct Christmas parties and other celebrations with a beautiful lady on his arm, *but never the same one twice.* There was no reason to suspect that with whom he had been dancing the previous evening would fare better than Sean's previous *amores.*

They talked for some 15 minutes, mostly about their two teenage children—a girl, Tiffany and her younger brother, Rob—and how they were doing in school. Then, fearing she'd be late for work as a construction manager with responsibilities overseeing several US government contracts, she blew Lou kisses, told him to watch his back, and said her goodbyes. Secretly, she said a little prayer to St. Michael the Archangel, Patron Saint of Police Officers, asking that he watch over her husband.

Lou dressed, packed his suitcase, stowed it in the trunk of their precinct's *Crown Vic,* and walked a short distance to Sean's room, where he knocked on the door.

O'Keeffe, dripping wet with a bath towel wrapped around his waist and a hairbrush in his right hand, opened the door and let Martelli in. He had a big smile on his face.

"Well, if it isn't NYPD's World Champion Ballroom Dancer, the one, the only, Detective Sean O'Keeffe!" Martelli deadpanned.

"Lou, we had the most fantastic time. And what a terrific dancer she is! It was magic. We danced on the terrace and watched the Moon set over the lake, turning the waves near the shore electric blue. If it wasn't for the fact she had to get up at 5:30 this morning, get her daughter off to school, and then do her rounds at the hospital, we would've danced until they closed."

Lou smiled. "I'm really happy for you, Sean. She seemed like a nice lady when I talked with her on the phone."

Sean walked back into the bathroom to finish drying off, comb his hair, and finish his morning ritual.

"Oh, Susan is. But life's dealt her some hard knocks. It hasn't been easy for her, believe me."

"In what way?"

"She lost her parents when she was 12 years old. They were killed in a boating accident, right here, on Lake George. Her aunt on her father's side raised her; the aunt was a professor at Albert Einstein College of Medicine in Manhattan. It's from her aunt that she gets her passion for medicine.

"After pre-med at the University of Wisconsin-Madison, she interned at Harvard followed by a residency at the University of Virginia. That's where she met her husband, who also was from upstate New York. They were married almost immediately, and their daughter, Heather, was born a year later. After they finished their residencies in Charlottesville, they returned to upstate New York and opened a practice together in Lake George."

"What happened to her husband?"

"He died three years ago. It was tragic. Turns out he volunteered two weeks of his time each year to provide free medical care to the indigenous peoples of Alaska. His plane went down near Chalkyitsik while on a mission to save a dying child. Both he and the pilot were killed."

"That must have been pretty rough on her."

Sean came out of the bathroom in his briefs and proceeded to dress.

"It was. But she had her daughter and the practice she and her husband had started, so she vowed to carry on. She's one tough woman, Lou. Reminds me a lot of Steph. Tough as nails on the outside, but sweet and loving on the inside. You know what I mean?"

"Oh, yes."

"You'll both get to meet her at the Christmas party this year. I'm going to drive up, and bring her and her daughter down—"

"Steph will be thrilled, Sean. Susan's daughter can stay with us. As for you and the doctor, you're on your own."

"Thanks, Lou. I knew I could count on you."

"Okay, let's get this show on the road. We'll grab a quick cup of coffee and a bagel up the road before meeting with the local sheriff at the vic's lake home."

Sean finished dressing, left the room key on the desk, finished packing his suitcase, and together with Martelli, left the room. Once they had stowed the suitcase in the trunk, Lou flipped Sean the keys to the *Crown Vic* and climbed into the passenger seat.

"Just keep your speed below 75, will you? The last thing you need is another encounter with Sergeant Logan. He won't be so forgiving next time."

"I haven't a clue as to what you're talking about, Lou."

"Let me rewind and play back some earlier events for you, my friend. As I recall, on our way up here from the city—you were driving, remember?—I asked how fast you were going. And you said: 'I don't know . . . maybe a 100, maybe 105, or so.'

"And I said, 'Maybe 105, or so? Are you out of your fucking mind?'

"And you responded by saying you wanted to blow out the engine. That's about the time when that New York State trooper—"

"Sergeant Logan."

"Yes, Sergeant Logan, pulled us over, and I told you to keep your hands on the steering wheel and play it cool."

"Oh, yeah, I remember now. You know what your problem is, Lou? You get your panties in a wad over the smallest of things. Speeding on the Interstate? That's chickenshit. Getting shot at like we did in Iraq, now, *that's* something to get concerned about."

"Yeah, well Logan didn't think it was such a small thing. He took it very seriously. So why did you have to pull his chain after he looked over your police identification, driver's license, and vehicle registration.

"What did I say? Sheesh, talk about someone getting up on the wrong side of the bed!"

"Oh, I see, my partner has a selective memory this morning. Recall, my fine feathered friend, what happened when he started to take out his ticket book, looked you straight in the eye, and, pointing his pen to his right, said, 'Detective, I have to tell you. I've been behind that clump of trees back there for the last two hours, just waiting for you.'

"What did you say to him?"

"Aaaah, let me think. Oh yes; I think it was something along the lines of: 'Well, Sergeant, I got here as quickly as I could.' "

"Bingo. And I was sitting there thinking: 'Holy crap, this guy will triple the fine and take us before a magistrate in some jerkwater town before he lets us go. Captain Hanlon down in our precinct will throw a shit fit!' "

"But that didn't happen, did it, Lou?"

"No, and lucky for you it didn't."

"But you know why nothing happened?" Sean continued. "The poor guy was thankful for anything that'd take his mind off the accident he had to clear before dawn yesterday morning. Remember how he described it. 'Horrible! Worst he'd ever seen. Three cars, nine people, including four children.' He knew one of the families. God-fearing people. He couldn't do anything for any of 'em. From the look of things, he said he thought they all died instantly. Made him wonder if this wasn't the time to hang up his gun and badge.

"Now, that's something *important*, Lou. You gotta learn to keep things in perspective. Like Logan. Remember what he said next?"

"Yeah, yeah, I remember," said Lou, obviously reluctant to acknowledge even the smallest nub of truth contained in Sean's logic. "He said, 'Okay, look, O'Keeffe, keep it under 80, would ya? I don't wanna have to scrape *you* and Martelli off the pavement like I did those kids this morning.' "

"See? There you go, Lou. It's all about priorities. Getting shot at changes them fast."

See Endnote 8.

"Solitude" (Photo: K. S. Brooks)
Indies Unlimited, December 18, 2021[7]

Just like old times, he thought, sitting alone on the vast
expanse of white sand that lay before him in southern New Mexico

---

7 Though the photo prompt is from Indies Unlimited's weekly competition for December 18, 2021, the story was too long to submit for competition. That said, I thank Ms. Brooks for inspiring me to present this tale. Inspiration also was drawn from a scene in Ted's mystery/thriller, *Eighth Circle: A Special Place in Hell*

9. Solitude

*J*ust like old times, he thought, sitting alone on the vast expanse of white sand that lay before him in southern New Mexico. Memories of Camp Udairi, Kuwait, flooded into his mind. In his ear, the sounds of Country Western music he "heard" reminded him of William "Bat" Masterson, his old Army buddy from Memphis, and the great music Masterson used to play on his CD player before the invasion of Iraq . . . songs by Alan Jackson, Lee Ann Womack and Willie Nelson, Faith Hill, Dolly Parton, and others. He and Bat used to sit and listen to Masterson's CDs for hours at a time after a full day of flying Black Hawks on practice missions over the Kuwaiti desert.

Martelli laughed softly, shaking his head. Now it all seemed a dream, and a bad one at that. *Closer to your worst nightmare*, he thought. *I was always amazed he'd even survived.*

What are you laughing about, Lou?

Martelli could hear Masterson's voice in his right ear, the ghost beside him.

Lou bit his lower lip. *Bat never made it back from Iraq*, he remembered. *I wonder whatever happened to his wife, Sherry, and their two boys.*

Masterson always was the first one in line for mail call, but the men never knew whether it was because of the sexy, perfumed love letters he got from Sherry or the Country Western CDs she included with every letter.

You were the lucky one, Lou, Masterson reminded Martelli, as if Lou needed reminding. Martelli had been aboard a Black Hawk helicopter that was shot down—a result of friendly fire, some thought—during the April 2003 invasion of Baghdad, a part of Operation Iraqi Freedom. Now, with the help of a prosthetic leg, he walked with a slight limp. He worked for NYPD under a special waiver issued by the mayor.

Hey, you're right, Bat, at least I'm alive. That's more than I can say for the pilot and copilot. He never talked about the fact that he lost his leg attempting to save them. His last memory before he blacked out was of their cries from the cockpit, desperate cries for help that he never was able to answer, desperate

47

cries that he heard over and over again in his nightmares until he thought he would go insane. It was Stephanie who always was there when that happened, soothing him, changing the bed sheets that had become drenched in sweat and assuring him that 'this too shall pass' and tomorrow would be a better day.

It was a miracle Martelli even made it into the Army. In grade school, while most of his friends were playing baseball or basketball after school or on weekends, Martelli was hustling to make a buck on the streets of Brooklyn and Manhattan. With his father Pietro, an NYPD street cop, working long hours on the Force and his mother taking odd jobs to keep the family in groceries, the boy had little in the way of supervision at home, day or night. It wasn't long before he was running numbers for local mobsters, hustling cards, working as a thimblerigger of a shell game on Broadway, picking pockets on the subway, and, in general, heading for a life of crime if not a long stay in prison, courtesy of the New York penal system.

Given the younger Martelli's behavior throughout his high school years, it should have come as no surprise when, immediately upon his graduation from high school, Pietro drove him to the Army recruiter's office and 'helped' him enlist. If anyone were to ask Louis today, he would tell them with that one act, his old man saved his life.

Still, those years on the street served the detective well, and when it came to cards and other games of chance as well as to 'reading' people, there were few who could be called his equal.

Martelli laughed again. *Boy, sitting in the goddamn desert waiting for someone to give us flying orders sure gave us plenty of time to learn the game of poker, didn't it, Bat?*

Learn? responded Masterson. *All we learned to do was cheat, for God's sake. I don't think we ever played an honest game!*

It was true. They all cheated, all the time. And they all knew it. But Martelli was the master when it came to dealing from the bottom of the deck, card culling, card segregation, card assembly, and forcing errors of judgment by badgering his opponents. This is what made their reunions such as the one tonight so much fun. Cheat, catch the other guys cheating, reminisce over old times, raise a bottle of beer to toast all who gave some in the war, and raise another bottle to toast those who gave all.[8]

As a Taylor Swift song "played" in Lou's ear, he rubbed the stub-left-leg upon which his prosthetic device was fitted. It felt like his toes were tingling. Which was strange because he had no toes on that leg. He did not even have a left foot. The fact was, he was missing his left leg from the knee down. Yet from time to time, he had these phantom sensations in which it felt like his toes were tingling, and these sensations usually occurred, for some strange reason, when a case was bothering him.

This time was no different. Even after all these years, he still hadn't been able to puzzle it out: why was he here and his best friend, William "Bat" Masterson, taken from his wife and two children? Why did bad things happen to good people like him while others less deserving were allowed to go on with their lives?

It didn't make sense. But then again, not much did since he first shipped out on deployment to the Middle East, lo those many years ago.

---

8 The phrase, 'All gave some . . . Some gave all,' was arguably first stated in a poem by the same title published in 2004 by Don Tyson.
http://www.authorsden.com/visit/viewPoetry.asp?id=94475

■ *Theodore Jerome Cohen*

"Teeter" (Photo: K. S. Brooks)
Indies Unlimited, January 22, 2022[9]

The shooter stopped at the casket, clasped his hands together,
bent slightly, teetered as if in prayer, straightened, turned to see
if anyone was watching, took something out of his pocket,
and placed it into the corpse's mouth.
is an example of his work.

---

[9] Though the photo prompt is from Indies Unlimited's weekly competition for December 25, 2021, the story was too long to submit for competition. That said, I thank Ms. Brooks for inspiring me to present this excerpt from my mystery/thriller, *Illth: Demon of the Night*. The book can be found on Amazon and other online booksellers, including B&N and Kobo. Note that the six books in the *Detective Louis Martelli NYPD Mystery/Thriller* Series can be read in any order.

10. Teeter

"Waddaya got for me, Missy?" Missy Dugan was a senior information technology specialist in 1 Police Plaza, or 1PP as the *cognoscenti* called it. She was busy reviewing the videotapes that had been recorded in the sanctuary of the Church of the Holy Redeemer on the previous afternoon at an unusual funeral service.

It now was 7 in the morning on the day after the funeral had been scheduled to take place. New York City Homicide Detective Louis Martelli had just come from his morning workout in Brooklyn's Dominant Fitness & Health Club. Weightlifting mixed with a strenuous aerobics program was the only way he could keep his 6-foot, 2-inch, 190-pound body from succumbing to the unhealthy food he often was forced to eat on the job.

"Antonetti finished his autopsy, he sent the slug to Ballistics. I have the results. As you might expect, it's copper-clad, not silver. I hope the garlic works, or we're in a heap of trouble!" She laughed.

"I wish Antonetti would keep his big mouth shut!"

"Well, it's not every day that someone puts a slug into a vampire, Lou."

Martelli scowled. "I could have told you it wasn't silver. It's too soft for use in ammunition. Unless you had a hard cast with low silver content, firing a silver bullet could really damage your firearm.

"So, were you able to match the slug to anything in the FBI's ballistics' database?"

"Yes. But it's not going to help you."

"I can't tell you how thrilled that makes me!" The exasperated look on his face was obvious.

"Well, I can tell you this . . . it was fired from a 9mm handgun. And—" She paused for impact. "The weapon was used to commit another murder a year ago, a murder that still hasn't been solved."

Martelli's eyes opened wide.

"Which case is that?"

"It's the Hayes shooting. Here, I pulled the file for you."

She took a folder from her workbench and handed it to him.

While Martelli leafed through the folder, Dugan filled him in. "The guy was found on the Upper West Side, face-down in Riverside Park near 103rd Street. You may not remember it because it was handled by the guys in the 24th Precinct. It didn't make much of a splash in the papers at the time because of some sex scandal involving a presidential candidate."

"They call that news?"

Martelli leafed through the file.

"Hmmm...one shot through the heart, close range. Looks pretty straightforward. The responding officer wrote it up as a robbery gone bad."

He set the file down and turned back to her. "I know it's early, but have you had a chance to review the videotapes from the church?"

"Of course, my liege. Some of us work while guys like you lounge around in a gym half the day, flexing your muscles and ogling the chicks!"

"Hey! I didn't have to come to work for this. If I wanted abuse, I would have stayed home!"

"Watch this." Missy swung her chair around and tapped several commands into her computer's keyboard. Instantly, one of several monitors lit up with the video taken by a camera that looked down on the altar from a vantage point near the ceiling of the sanctuary.

"The time is around 12:13 PM. What you're looking at is a shot of the funeral director and one of his men wheeling the casket in for the service, which probably was supposed to start around 1 PM."

"Okay, I see that."

"There . . . the casket's in position." Missy pointed at the monitor. "And here comes a man with a cart containing flowers."

"Right," agreed Martelli. "And now the other two men are opening the casket, making final adjustments to the lining and the corpse's hands, straightening out the lining around the deceased's shoes—by the way, never look down there, Missy . . . it's where the viscera bag is stored—and so forth. Nothing appears to be out of the ordinary."

"I agree . . . looks like business as usual."

Martelli and Dugan watched the screen in silence as the men went about their work.

Finally, Missy spoke. "Okay, looks like everything's ready. See? The men are leaving the sanctuary."

The date-time display on the screen showed a time of 12:34 pm.

"They're probably going outside to grab a sandwich or smoke, Lou. Note that no one is in the camera's field of view. I checked all of the other cameras as well. There's not a person in the sanctuary at this time. But then—"

"Wait! What's that in the corner, Missy?"

Missy started to laugh. "That, my friend, is the shooter."

The screen showed someone who appeared to be a man entering the large, raised platform that stretched across the front of the church and upon which the altar stood. Dressed in a long priest's robe and wearing a black, low-crowned, wide-brimmed ecclesiastical hat, he emerged slowly from behind the curtains at the far, left back of the platform, as one viewed the sanctuary from the rear. After looking around to ensure no one was in the sanctuary, he walked down the stairs, and at the bottom, turned left and quickly made his way toward the casket.

"I can't see his face, Missy! Where the hell did he come from?"

"I checked some of our surveillance cameras on the streets around the church. One caught a shot of him walking into the small cemetery behind the building and entering through the service entrance. But that's about all I can tell you. Now, watch closely."

The shooter stopped at the casket, clasped his hands together, bent slightly, teetered as if in prayer, straightened, turned to see if anyone was watching, took something out of his pocket, and placed it into the corpse's mouth.

"That must have been the garlic you found, Lou."

"Right, and now he's screwing the silencer onto the gun barrel."

"I see that."

They watched as the shooter pushed the silencer against the side of the casket and pulled the trigger.

Martelli shook his head. "Bada-bing bada-boom, right through the casket into the corpse."

They continued watching intently as the shooter retraced his footsteps across the sanctuary floor, climbed the stairs to the platform, and continued through the curtains to make his escape, most probably using the same service entrance through which he had entered.

"Were you able to track him on his way off the church's property?"

"Not very far. We don't have a lot of cameras in that area. And to make things worse, at some point he probably shed the priest's garb and either stuck it in a bag or dumped it."

"Okay, go back and grab the best screen shot of the shooter you can get and e-mail it to CSU."

"10-4."

Martelli reached for the phone on Dugan's workbench and dialed the Department's Crime Scene Unit.

"NYPD CSU, Sergeant Reynolds."

"Reynolds, this is Martelli of the First."

"Hey, Lou, long time no see. How are you and the family?"

"Good, Adam. And you and yours?"

"Great. How can I help you?"

"We had a shooting yesterday at a church in the First. Some guy pumped a round into a corpse."

"I know. What the hell is that all about?"

"Beats the shit out of me."

"Man, it's getting weird out there, Lou."

"Tell me about it. Listen, Dugan is e-mailing you a screen shot of the shooter. It's not great, but it's the best we have. The perp—and we're assuming it's a man—disguised himself as a priest. He was dressed in a long robe and wore a black, low-crowned, wide-brimmed ecclesiastical hat."

"Okay."

"Could you send a CSU team back to the church to search for additional evidence? Perhaps your people'll be able to lift a print or two from the inside and outside knobs of the door at the service entrance. Or, in showing the screen shot to people in the neighborhood, maybe they'll find someone who can tell them in which direction he walked. In the best of all worlds, we might even get a better description of the person or an ID, but I doubt it."

"I'll take care of it, Lou. Are you considering putting out a BOLO for the guy?"

"No. We don't have enough information to go on yet. And the guy isn't going to be walking around in that get-up, that's for sure. All we need is for our people to be questioning every man of the cloth they encounter on the street, and we'll have the Catholic Church all over us. If that happens, you know the media . . . they'll blow the whole thing way out of proportion."

"Like they do everything else."

"Right. That would make our job even more difficult than it already is."

"Yeah, I know what you mean. Used to be you could trust them, but today, most are just out to make a quick name for themselves. Anyway, I'll send a unit to the church now."

"Thanks, Adam. I owe you!"

"Don't mention it, Lou."

Martelli returned the handset to its cradle and turned his attention back to Dugan.

"Okay, Missy, did Antonetti have anything else to say?"

"Yeah, he said to tell you to stop at the Korean grocer's on your way home tonight, buy some garlic, and hang it around your neck. He said you can't be too careful these days, especially when there might be vampires prowling Gotham City at night."

"Well, isn't he just a barrel of laughs! Listen, NYPD needs this case like a hole in the head . . . chasing what someone wants the Department to think is the 'killer' of vampires, werewolves, and other forms of lowlife."

Missy could barely stifle a grin. "Don't you mean 'no-life,' Martelli?"

Despite himself, Martelli had to laugh. "Give me a break, will ya?

"What else did the 'court jester' have to say?"

"Actually, he said he wanted to see you this morning after you're done here. Even though there had been a cursory autopsy performed on the deceased at the time of his death, something important turned up."

"What was it?"

"He wouldn't tell me . . . he just said he wanted to see you when we finished here."

"The City Below" (Photo: K. S. Brooks)
Indies Unlimited, January 29, 2022[10]

BROOKLYN, MARTELLI BEDROOM - EARLY MORNING

---

10 Because of a previous WIN earlier this month, Ted is not eligible to enter a story for the weekly Flash Fiction competition (except for the purpose of competing for an Editor's Choice Award).

11. The City Below

March, 2010, 3 a.m. –
The city below, as seen from the Martelli's bedroom window. Sound of distant thunder; occasional lightning illuminates two sleeping adults. Suddenly, a blinding lightning strike is followed instantly by loud clap of thunder.

NIGHTMARE and MARTELLI FLASHBACK

Burning Black Hawk down in Iraq. Rounds going off. Blinding flashes of light. Audible, Klaxon-like alarm. Figure standing in cargo doorway is Crew Chief, Master Sergeant Louis MARTELLI. Flames everywhere. MARTELLI motions frantically to PILOT and CO-PILOT to get out.

                    MARTELLI
Come on!
                    PILOT (O.S.)
          (screaming)
Can't move! Get out! Get out!

MARTELLI moves towards cockpit and screaming pilots when explosion throws him back towards open cargo door, shattering his left leg. He struggles to his feet, only to be blown out the cargo door by blast.

CLOSE ON MARTELLI'S face as Klaxon-like sound morphs to vibrating, buzzing cell phone on bed stand. Lightning illuminates his face. Frantic, sweating, dirty -- same as on battlefield.

Wife STEPHANIE barely moves.

MARTELLI flips open cell phone.

> MARTELLI
> (in pain memory)
> Martelli!

> NYPD CENTRAL DISPATCH (V.O.)
> Get down to the Financial District.
> ANTONETTI will meet you there – at The
> *Wall Street Bull*!

> MARTELLI
> I'm on it.

MARTELLI terminates the call. Lightening illuminates his service revolver, NYPD badge, and a prosthetic leg on the bed stand. STEPHANIE reaches out and touches his shoulder.

> STEPHANIE
> You okay?

> MARTELLI
>
> I'm fine, Steph. Something's come up. I gotta
> go.

Gets up, and hops to the bathroom with his service revolver, badge, and prosthetic leg.

EXT. MANHATTAN, FINANCIAL DISTRICT, THE *WALL STREET BULL* -
CONTINUOUS

MARTELLI brings his unmarked Ford *Crown Vic* to the curb. The red light from his portable, roof-mounted strobe lamp reflects off the blood on the pavement beneath the head of the *Wall Street Bull*. We see a head spiked to the left horn. MARTELLI uses both hands to lift his left leg over car's door frame. Walks to the *Bull*.

> MARTELLI
> (bellowing)
> Well, what do we have here, Michael?

Michael ANTONETTI is standing on a short step ladder, working around a human head. The words 'Deputy Coroner' are emblazoned on his jacket. An NYPD CSI is taking photographs.

> ANTONETTI
> What do we have? What the hell does it look like
> we have? It's the Running of the fucking Bulls in
> Pamplona, for Christ's sake!

> MARTELLI
> Boy, I guess if you live long enough, you'll see it
> all.

MARTELLI looks at his watch.

> MARTELLI (CONT'D)
> (yawns)
> Damn. I'd rather be in bed with my wife --
> while the kids are still asleep, if you catch my
> drift. So--

> ANTONETTI
> Before you ask, no, we don't have a body.

FLASHBACK

FLASH FRAMES CLOSE ON shadows of one man coming up behind another man, thrusting his left arm around victim, injecting a syringe into neck with his right hand, and dropping the victim to pavement.

MARTELLI
And the head is--

FLASHBACK
FLASH FRAMES CLOSE ON killer decapitating victim.

ANTONETTI
Sliced off nice and clean, just like whoever did it was butchering a hog. The body, I suspect, has been sliced and diced, with the pieces thrown in either the East or Hudson River.

FLASHBACK
FLASH FRAMES CLOSE ON killer throwing weighted black plastic bag into river and reaching for another.

MARTELLI
How long would you say it's been here?

ANTONETTI
No more than an hour. The surveillance cameras in the area should give you the time and maybe, even, a look at who created this bit of modern art.

MARTELLI
Any clue on the vic?

ANTONETTI
Not from what we have. The patrolman over there spotted the head when he drove by 20

minutes ago. But the guy on the curb – the one who's puking his guts out -- may know the vic.

MARTELLI pulls a notebook from the inside pocket of his suit coat and limps towards man hunched over curb. He is Steve JACOBS, a man in his late 20s with an expensive taste in clothes.

> **MARTELLI**
> So, do you always make it a practice of being down here this early?

JACOBS looks up through bloodshot eyes. He does not respond.

> **MARTELLI (CONT'D)**
> I'm detective Lou Martelli, Manhattan Homicide. Whatever happened to your friend -- I'm assuming he was a friend -- occurred within the last hour or so. The best thing you can do to help us catch whoever was responsible is tell me as much as you can, as quickly as you can.

JACOBS slowly rises to his feet and wipes his mouth with a handkerchief.

> **JACOBS**
> You're right. I'm sorry. My name's Steve Jacobs. I worked with John...John Williamson.

JACOBS points to the head on the statue. Gags.

> **JACOBS (CONT'D)**
> He's ... he was ... my boss at Bartlett, Cline, and Stephenson. It's a securities firm. I was coming in early to catch up on my work.

MARTELLI

I hear ya ... not enough hours in the day! So, when was the last time you saw Williamson alive?

JACOBS

We had dinner late last night at Capricious. It's just down--

MARTELLI

I know where it is. What time did you leave?

JACOBS

Around 11. I used valet parking. John had parked his car down the street somewhere, so we said goodbye at the restaurant. That's the last time I saw him.

MARTELLI

What was he driving?

JACOBS

A Ferrari 599 GTB Fiorano. Red.

MARTELLI

And the license number?

JACOBS

It's a New York vanity plate ... easy to remember. It says SAVE.

MARTELLI

SAVE?

JACOBS

He told me it was a joke on the 'little people,' the ones who no matter how much they saved, would never even come close to 'making it' big.

MARTELLI gives that 'what a jerk' look, grabs a handheld radio from his waist, and keys up the transmitter.

>   MARTELLI
> First Squad to Central

>   CENTRAL DISPATCH
>   (V.O./RADIO)
> Go to First

>   MARTELLI
> 10-10 on the following vehicle wanted in connection with a homicide investigation, vehicle is a red 2010 Ferrari 599 GTB Fiorano bearing New York tag number Sierra, Alpha, Victor, Echo, last seen in the area of Broadway and Morris Street in Manhattan. Request a citywide BOLO.

>   CENTRAL DISPATCH
>   (V.O./RADIO)
> 10-4, First.

MARTELLI turns his attention back to JACOBS.

>   MARTELLI
> Do you know of anyone who might have held a grudge against Mr. Williamson?

>   JACOBS
> I can't think of anyone.

MARTELLI

Girlfriends? Boyfriends of those girlfriends?
Maybe someone he owed money to?

JACOBS

I didn't know the people he hung with. Except
for work and an occasional lunch or late-night
dinner, we never saw each other.

MARTELLI

Yeah? What did you talk about at dinner?

JACOBS

Oh, the usual. I'm a mid-level stock analyst. I
worked with John covering a bunch of biotechs.
John was the senior analyst. He told me the
position we would take when writing a report ...
you know, BUY, HOLD, SELL.

MARTELLI

(scrutinizes him)
You two didn't have a falling out, did you?

JACOBS

(now scared)
What? Look, he was the senior analyst -- just
told me what to do. You don't think I killed
him?

MARTELLI

Here's my card. Go to work and let them know
what's happened. Tell them you're going to
have to come down to my office later this

morning to meet with me. Now, give me your driver's license and business card.

JACOBS
(shaky voice)
Detective, I don't know why anyone would want to--

MARTELLI
Please do what I asked.

JACOBS beats a hasty retreat to his car. MARTELLI returns to the scene.

MARTELLI (CONT'D)
I'm leaving, Michael. Let me have a copy of your report as soon as possible, please.

ANTONETTI gives him the 'when it's done' look.

ANTONETTI
I'll say this ... given all the cameras we have around here, whoever did this must have been really angry ... and organized. They'd have to be to dump the vic's head here.

See Endnote 9.

"Progress" (Photo: K. S. Brooks)
Indies Unlimited, April 16, 2022[11]

**Management's intent was to build a dedicated building to meet
an ever-increasing demand for pediatric care.**

---

11 Though the photo prompt is from Indies Unlimited's weekly competition
for April 16, 2022, the story was too long to submit for competition. That said,
I thank Ms. Brooks for inspiring me to present this tale.

12. Progress

The selected *Times* archived webpage, having opened, revealed an article from a year earlier. The headline read: **Hospital Fights Developers Over Land Rezoning.**

"Looks like the hospital's Board of Directors is locked in a ferocious battle with several local real estate developers and the city over the rezoning of the land adjacent to the hospital," observed Detective Louis "Lou" Martelli as he and the department's Principal IT Specialist Missy Dugan read the *Times*

The two continued reading as Missy scrolled the screen display. The land, now vacant, previously had been the site of a multi-story apartment building razed by the owner in 2011. He intended to sell the land to the hospital. To this end, the hospital's management was seeking zoning for the vacant property consistent with the hospital's current land-use permit. Management's intent was to build a dedicated building to meet an ever-increasing demand for pediatric care. To the hospital's relief, the New York City Department of City Planning, on a "Sense of the Department vote" early in 2013, indicated its support for the institution's petition. "Guess that's what you call progress," she observed dryly.

However, the fact that the land was located in close proximity to the Chambers Street stations for the 1, 2, 3 and for the A, C, and E subway lines made the property highly valuable to major New York and New Jersey developers, several of whom were fighting both with the hospital and the Department of City Planning to have the land zoned for commercial use such that the variances obtained would permit them to build a tower office building. Not surprisingly, after the informal Department vote, there were accusations the mayor had favored the hospital's zoning petition, a result not only of his granddaughter-in-law's condition and of her being treated in that facility, but also, because he had given, and now gave, generously to the institution.

In fact, the mayor previously had favored the developers. However, more recently, he not only had recused himself from any involvement in the deliberations surrounding the rezoning applications but also had named a bipartisan panel to act as a consultant to the Department of City Planning in the matter.

Still, according to the *Times* article, the mayor's office could not shake the taint of scandal. Was money being exchanged under the table? If so, who were the sources and who were the recipients? More to the point, was the mayor on the take? Were members of the Department of City Planning involved? What kind of negotiations were going on behind closed doors? Was the public fully apprised of the conflicts of interest among the parties involved?

Despite repeated attempts by the *Times* and other city papers to pierce the veil of secrecy, little was known of the decision-making process. And with no decision made—and hundreds of millions of dollars in development money hanging in the balance—tempers were fraying.

Some were calling for the New York Attorney General and the United States Attorney for the Southern District of New York to initiate investigations in the matter. But the questions were: Investigate who? Investigate what? No zoning decision had been made. There was no evidence of malfeasance. There was not even the hint of circumstantial evidence to support a claim of corruption. It all boiled down to rumor, innuendo, and gossip.

Martelli and Dugan looked at each other.

"Whaddaya think, Lou?"

"Treacherous waters, to be sure. Plenty of room for fraud and abuse. Whoever wins, we're talking a multi-year construction effort worth thousands of jobs, huge steel, concrete, and glass contracts, not to mention the costs associated with the installation of HVAC, plumbing, and electrical services. And that's all before the owners, whoever they eventually are, even open the doors for business.

"The question is: Would that make someone want to kill two people—specifically, the mayor's grandson and his wife—two people who ostensibly have no interest in such an undertaking? And if so, why?"

See Endnote 10.

"Shackleford's Lament" (Photo: damrong, Big Stock Photo)

Shackleford took the cigarette from his mouth and
flicked the ash into a half-filled ashtray.

13. Shackleford's Lament

Martelli had not even reached the door of John Shackleford office in the basement of 1PP the next morning when he knew, by the sound of the man's persistent, hacking smoker's cough, the parole officer was already hard at work.

"John, are you still smoking two packs a day? I thought that stuff would have killed you by now."

Cigarette smoke hung in the air, giving the room a bluish cast. Both the city and the wheezing air purifier in the corner had attempted mightily to address the parole officer's smoking problem with equal lack of success. Adding to the gloomy atmosphere were the lack of a window and two overhead fluorescent lamps, one of which was flickering. *This guy's office looks like the set from a 1930's detective flick*, thought Martelli.

As was the case with the Martelli's office, files were strewn everywhere, many piled to heights of two feet or more. If there was a telephone on the man's desk, even he would have been hard pressed to find it.

The parole officer looked up and smiled. A cigarette with half an inch of ash perched on the end dangled from his lips. "Well I'll be go to Hell, if it isn't Detective-Investigator Louis Martelli of the First."

Shackleford, a thin, wiry man, was five-five in height and dressed in clothes that looked like they came from a thrift shop. His suit jacket, which reeked of cigarette smoke, was brown and hung loosely from his body. His pants were of the same color and at least an inch too long. Not that this did not serve a purpose, that being to cover his shoes, also brown, which had not seen polish in several months.

Shackleford took the cigarette from his mouth, flicked the ash into a half-filled ashtray, and then, using the little finger and thumb of his left hand, carefully picked a small piece of tobacco from the tip of his tongue.

"Nasty stuff. Don't ever start smoking, Martelli." He wagged a nicotine-stained finger at the detective. "Take it from me. It's a dirty, expensive habit."

73

With that, he took one last drag on his cigarette, rubbed the butt out in the ashtray, and taking a fresh cigarette—the last—from the spent pack on his desk, lit it, sat back, put his hands behind his head, and blew a perfect smoke ring into the air, watching it as it floated slowly toward the ceiling.

"So, how can this humble public servant help the First Precinct this fine morning?"

"I'm guessing here, John, but might you be the lucky winner of the Niccolo Prosperi Lottery?"

Shackleford sat straight up and snuffed out the cigarette he had just lit. "That piece of shit. That son of a bitch! He was supposed to sign in with me two weeks ago, and I ain't seen hide nor hair of him. Further, the address he gave the parole board upon release is bogus. A total fucking fraud.

"Now the guy's gone off the grid. He's out of Sing Sing three weeks, and he's already violated his parole! Believe me, we're looking for him!

"So, what's your interest in the guy, Lou?"

"Well, we have good reason to believe he's the one who torched my wife's car the other night."

"Really? I read about that in the paper. Scary shit. What the hell are you involved in that would make someone hire Prosperi to come after you?"

"That's what I want to know. Meantime, I got a tip this guy Prosperi might have been—"

Martelli was interrupted by his cell phone ringing. He held his left forefinger in the air. "Hold on a second, John." Martelli pulled the phone from his suit jacket's right pocket and looked at the screen. "It's Ray Preston, Arson and Explosion Squad."

Shackleford nodded his understanding. Taking a new pack of cigarettes from his desk drawer, he smacked it on the palm of his left hand several times, opened the pack, carefully extracted one cigarette, and popping it between his lips, lit it using a small disposable lighter.

Meanwhile, Martelli had taken the call. "Yes, Ray."

"Lou, I just e-mailed the list I promised you. We identified ten persons of interest having the signature of your arsonist. But as far as I know, they're all behind bars."

"Is Niccolo Prosperi on your list?"

"Why yes. How did you come up with *his* name?"

"I got a tip last night from an informant. You *do* know, of course, Prosperi was released from Sing Sing three weeks ago and has gone missing. I'm with his parole officer now. He has no idea where the man is, but they're already searching for him."

"Damn, Louis, he certainly didn't waste any time finding employment. Let me know if there's anything I can do to help you. Meanwhile, I'll put out feelers and see if anyone's picked up any chatter on the guy."

"Thanks, Ray."

Martelli ended the call and returned his cell phone to his suit jacket pocket.

"Anyway, John, as you heard, I got a tip last night Prosperi might be our guy. And now, he turns up on Preston's short list of likely candidates based on his *modus operandi*."

"So, what are you going to do, Lou?"

"Well, someone hired him to do that job on Steph's car. He didn't just pull the idea out of his ass. So, the first thing is to contact the people at Sing Sing and see who contacted him in the weeks prior to his release."

"Great! And when you find that bastard Prosperi, put him away for a long, long time. I don't ever want to have to think about him again!"

See Endnote 11.

"The Pier" (K. S. Brooks)
Indies Unlimited, February 12, 2022[12]

**The area around Hudson River Pier 63 on West 23rd Street
has a long and interesting history.**

---

12 Though the photo prompt is from Indies Unlimited's weekly competition
for February 12, 2022, the story was too long to submit for competition. That
said, I thank Ms. Brooks for inspiring me to write this tale.

14. Pier

The area around Hudson River Pier 63 on West 23rd Street[13] has a long and interesting history, one as old and storied as New York City itself. Dating from the time of the Lenape Indian Tribe in the early 15th through the early 17th centuries, the area was an important center both for Indian life and trading. But it was not until the early 1800s that the waterfront began to grow rapidly, a result of the completion of the Erie Canal. By 1874, the city's Department of Docks constructed the first masonry bulkhead at Christopher Street—the continuation of 9th Street to the west of its intersection with Sixth Avenue. The docks soon were built out in rapid succession, with the bow notch at Pier 45 in Greenwich Village the last effort made to accommodate the cruise ships from the major lines that used North River as the embarkation point for their journeys.[14] Interestingly, Pier 63 was only nine blocks from Pier 54, where on April 18, 1912, the *Carpathia* docked with 709 survivors of the *Titanic* disaster.

Thoughts of his father, Pietro, a street cop who had died years earlier after being ambushed near a warehouse on the dock that he now was approaching, flooded into his mind as he pulled onto to the pier and parked. He thought of his mother, Claudia, who never was the same after his father was laid to rest. Many who knew her said they saw the light go out of her eyes when the last shovelful of dirt was spread on his grave.

Still, he smiled as he made his way toward the river. His emotions were driven by a comforting thought derived from something only he knew. Every year, on the anniversary of his father's death, he went to the waterfront near the warehouse where his father died, threw a wreath of fresh white flowers into the Hudson River, said a prayer, and shed tears for a man called to his

---

13 Pier 40 is located at Houston Street, and the numbering of the piers to the north correspond to the nearest numbered street plus 40.

14 Source: Friends of Hudson River Park & Hudson River Park Trust

Lord years before his time. Neither his wife nor their children knew about this. It was something he did as a private celebration of his father's life and a way of ensuring his father's memory would survive as long as *he* was alive.

Like my father, he thought, *I am many persons, and even those who love me may never know them all.*[15]

---

15 This is an excerpt from Ted's fifth Detective Louis Martelli novel, *Eighth Circle: A Special Place in Hall.*

"Lunch" (Photo: K.S. Brooks)
Indies Unlimited, October 29, 2022[16]

**On the left, in the far corner of the porch,
the men could see a dining area.**

---

16 Though the photo prompt is from Indies Unlimited's weekly competition
for October 29, 2022, the story was too long to submit for competition. That
said, I thank Ms. Brooks for inspiring me to present this tale.

15. Lunch

"**W**ell, if it isn't Sheriff Ward. How are you, Geoff?"

"Just fine, Diane. Thanks for asking. This here is Detective Louis Martelli of the New York Police Department. We were wondered if you might have a little time to answer a few questions regarding Phil Weston."

She smiled broadly. "Of course, of course. Please come in. It's so nice to have company."

Goodman, a widow, was in her mid-70s. Short, with gray hair, she was more than a few pounds overweight. 'I'm big boned,' is what she told her closest friends when they would discuss their weight problems while playing Mahjongg on Wednesday afternoons. Goodman was dressed in a bright rainbow-striped housecoat and smelled as if she had just taken a scented bath.

She stepped back, motioning them onto the porch that encircled the lower level of the house on three sides. On the left, in the far corner, the men could see a dining area. It appeared Diane was about to start lunch.

A couch was positioned to the right of the dining table, the first of several pieces of furniture that Goodman and her guests used when they read or simply relaxed while enjoying a refreshing lake breeze.

To the right was a door that led to the cottage's kitchen while next to it, another led to the living room.

"Gentlemen . . . please . . . go into the living room. I'll join you in a minute. How do you take your coffee?"

"I'll take mine with milk, Diane."

"Fine, Geoff. And you, Detective?"

"Please call me Lou, Diane. I take mine black . . . straight up."

"Okay, Lou. I'll be back in a minute. Please, make yourselves at home."

Diane picked up her cup of soup and disappeared into the kitchen. The sheriff and Martelli let themselves into the living room. It was an anachronism. The year may have been 2011 but the room was painted and

81

decorated as if it were as early as the mid-1930s but certainly not much later than the outbreak of World War II. The walls and ceiling were painted light beige while large, thick, Persian carpets covered the hardwood floor. A darkly stained upright piano stood next to the stairs leading to the second floor, which housed three small bedrooms and a bathroom. Opulent chairs, carefully positioned around a coffee table in the center of the living room, were covered in vintage brocade fabrics while several display cabinets filled with family pictures and porcelain artifacts lined two windowless walls. Appropriately placed end tables covered with knick-knacks and tchotchkes rounded out the room's furnishings.

Wow, thought Martelli, *for all intents and purposes, time has stood still. This room hasn't changed in 75 years.*

"Here you are, gentleman. Geoff, I'll let you pour your own milk. And I brought something for us to nosh on while we talk. Just don't tell Dr. Allerton I ate any of these."

She set a plate of homemade cinnamon rolls on the coffee table. "She's been warning me about my blood sugar level, so I'm trying to cut back on my sweets. But I still cheat a little, now and then." She put the forefinger of her right hand over her lips.

Martelli picked right up on what she was saying. "Your secret is safe with me, Diane."

She giggled.

"This really is a beautiful home you have," he continued, attempting to break the ice.

"It was given to my father by his uncle in the early 1950s. They worked together during World War II. When the uncle retired to Florida, he gave my father this home in exchange for one dollar. We used it as a summer home until my father died in 1967, and then, my mother and I lived in it until she died in 2005. Now I have it. It's just like it always was. Nothing's changed."

Martelli smiled. "I imagine that's a great comfort to you."

"Not everything has to change, Lou. It's possible to find happiness even in the simplest of things . . . a cool lake breeze, fireflies on a hot summer night, a spring thunderstorm. They are as enjoyable and comforting to me now as they were in 1953."

She smiled, closed her eyes momentarily, and nodded. Then she turned and stared out through the room's large picture window, across, and beyond, to the lake, as if in her mind's eye she still could see her family as they were when she was a little girl. Slowly she turned back to look at the men.

"Well, Detective, you didn't come all this way to hear me talk about this house and my family. How can I help you?"

"Diane, I can't go into too much detail because of the nature of my investigation, but I will tell you your neighbor, Mr. Weston, did *not* die of natural causes."

Goodman stopped sipping her reheated soup and stared at Martelli. "What?"

"I know this will come as a shock. We don't know who killed him. Nor do we have a motive."

Goodman swallowed, then, sat silently, attempting to make sense of something that clearly made no sense to her. Slowly, she wiped her mouth with a linen napkin.

"I can't believe it."

The men let what Martelli had just told her sink in.

Finally, the sheriff spoke. "Diane, if there's anything you can remember about Phil regarding the last few days before his death, it could be of immense importance to our investigation."

"Well, let me think. Phil and I never spoke, of course. Never had any reason to. Years ago, he made it crystal clear that he wasn't interested in establishing any kind of neighborly relationship with me. Occasionally, I'd see him talking to Arnold Braun—he's another strange one, that Braun fellow— but even those exchanges appeared to have petered out a while back."

Sheriff Ward picked up the conversation. "Did Phil have any visitors over the years that you recall, Diane?"

"Let's see. Oh, yes, several years ago there was a couple and their daughter who came to visit him in the summer. If I remember correctly, they were here two or three times . . . always in the middle of July. But they didn't show up last year. Nor did I see the family this year."

"Are you sure about that, Diane?"

83

"Oh, yes. Other than that couple and their child, no one ever came to see Phil. Their visits aren't something I would forget."

"Do you remember anything about them? For example, what did they look like? What kind of car did they drive? Anything at all?"

"Well, they weren't Caucasians, if that's what you mean."

"How so?" asked Martelli.

"Their skin seemed darker. And their features were different. They could have been Middle Eastern."

"And their car? Do you know the make?"

"What do I know? My father always drove a Packard *Clipper* . . . the last one was turquoise and white with big whitewall tires. Now, *that* was a real car, not like the junk they sell today."

Martelli laughed. "I take that as a 'no.'"

Goodman laughed. "Your mother didn't raise no dumb kid, Lou. But I can tell you this. The man showed up over there—alone—the day before Phil was found dead, and he wasn't driving the same car he drove when his family—at least I think it was his family—came to Phil's on earlier visits. The car he drove this time was small and gray; when he came with his family, he drove a larger car . . . one of those, what do they call them? Oh, yes . . . SUVs. And that one was white."

Martelli was busy taking notes as Sheriff Ward asked the next question. "How long did he stay this time?"

"Oh, maybe 20 minutes, 25 minutes, tops. Which surprised me, because before, when the three of them came to visit, they always stayed a couple of hours. Anyway, I was puttering around the porch when I saw him pull Phil's front door shut. Then, he turned and walked to his car—"

"Did he appear to be in a hurry?"

"Not particularly. He threw his briefcase in the back seat, got in the driver's seat, started the engine, and drove away. I didn't think anything of it."

Martelli thought for a minute. "If I brought an artist up here, Diane, is it possible the two of you might be able to come up with a sketch of the man?"

"I doubt it, Lou. Not that I wouldn't be willing to give it a try, but I only saw the side of the man's head, and from quite a distance at that."

"Okay, I understand. Just one or two more questions, then. Could you venture a guess as to the age of the people in the family? We understand there also was a child . . . a girl."

"Well, when I last saw the woman, which was two years ago, I'd say she was in her early 30s. The little girl could not have been more than 4 years old at the time. I don't know . . . she looked very young and frail."

"And the man?"

"I'd say he was in his mid- to late 30s."

The men finished their cinnamon rolls and coffee, wiped their mouths, and stood up.

Goodman looked up at them. "Anything else I can do for you, gentlemen?"

"Well," said Martelli, "I sure could use a bathroom."

"I'll second that," said the sheriff."

"It's at the top of the stairs, on your right. But don't flush the toilet until you've both used it! I'm on a well here. If you both flush, you'll stir up the sand at the bottom of the well, and then, I'll have problems with my pump!"

See Endnote 12.

"Need for Speed" (Photo: K.S. Brooks)
Indies Unlimited, November 13, 2022[17]

"Lou, I have a New York State trooper on my tail."

---

17 Though the photo prompt is from Indies Unlimited's weekly competition for November 13, 2022, the story was too long to submit for competition. That said, I thank Ms. Brooks for inspiring me to present this tale.

16. Need for Speed

"Lou, I have a New York State trooper on my tail."

"How fast were you going?"

"I don't know . . . maybe a 100, maybe 105, or so."

"Maybe 105, or so? Are you out of your freaking mind?"

"Well, I wanted to blow out the engine."

"Pull over. And for God's sake, keep your hands on the steering wheel."

"Oh, don't get your panties in a wad. He can see we're cops." Having done two tours of duty in Iraq, NYPD Detective Sean O'Keeffe often told people getting shot at quickly changes one's priorities.

"Just roll down your window and keep your hands on the wheel, Sean," hissed Detective Lou Martelli.

The state trooper, his car roof lights flashing, pulled his dark blue sedan behind the detective's car and stopped. He sat in his vehicle for a few minutes, obviously communicating with State Police Headquarters via a high-speed digital radio link regarding the make and model as well as the license number of the NYPD *Crown Vic* in front of him. When he was finished, he got out of his car, holstered his night stick, put on his wide-brimmed hat, and walked to where O'Keeffe and Martelli sat. They could see he carried the rank of sergeant. His name tag read 'Logan.'

"Good morning, gentlemen. Driver's license and registration, please."

O'Keeffe handed the trooper his NYPD leather badge holder and identification, driver's license, and vehicle registration.

"Well, well, well. What do we have here? One of New York City's Finest?"

The officer examined the three items, nodding his head as he looked first at O'Keeffe's police identification, then at the detective's driver's license, and finally, at the vehicle's registration papers.

Then, as he started to take out his ticket book, he looked O'Keeffe straight in the eye, and pointing his pen to his right, said, "Detective, I have to tell you. I've been behind that clump of trees back there for the last two hours, just waiting for you."

O'Keeffe, nonplussed, didn't skip a beat. "Well, Sergeant, I got here as quickly as I could."

Holy shit, thought Martelli. *This guy will triple the fine and take us before a magistrate in some jerkwater town before he lets us go. Captain Hanlon will throw a shit fit!*

For a moment the officer just stared at him, and then broke into a wide grin and laughed. "I needed that, O'Keeffe."

Martelli raised his eyes to the Heavens. *Thank you, Lord.*

"This has been one crappy day, Detective, I can tell you that. I'm thankful for anything that'll take my mind off the accident I had to clear before dawn this morning. It was horrible . . . three cars, nine people, including four children. I knew one of the families . . . they were good God-fearing people. I couldn't do anything for any of 'em. From the look of things, they died instantly. Made me wonder if this wasn't the time to hang up my gun and badge, and start my own home security firm."

He looked away for a few seconds, nodded as if he were saying to himself, "*Yes, maybe that's what I'll do,*" then turned his gaze back to O'Keeffe.

"So, what takes you guys so far out of your jurisdiction?"

Martelli leaned over and flashed his badge. "Martelli, here, Sarge. We're on our way to Lake George . . . murder investigation. Originally, we thought the vic died of natural causes, but it turned out he was poisoned by someone who injected him with snake venom. He suffocated to death, though he may have suffered a heart attack at the same time. So now, we and the sheriff up there have a problem. Who, what, when, where, and why?"

"Well, at least you got the *how* covered. It never stops, does it, guys?

"Okay, look, O'Keeffe, keep it under 80, would ya? I don't wanna have to scrape you off the pavement like I did those kids this morning."

"You got it, Sarge. And thanks."

See Endnote 13.

"Disrepair" (Photo: K.S. Brooks)
Indies Unlimited, November 27, 2022[18]

Martelli doubted he would find grass under the soggy leaves that covered the land, not because the houses were old and in disrepair, but simply because most had no occupants to care for the grounds.

---

18 Though the photo prompt is from Indies Unlimited's weekly competition for November 27, 2022, the story was too long to submit for competition. That said, I thank Ms. Brooks for inspiring me to present this tale.

17. Disrepair

Martelli pulled his unmarked *Crown Vic* to the curb in one of Brooklyn's oldest residential neighborhoods, turned off the ignition, and surveyed the scene around him. He imagined in his mind's eye how the block must have looked 'back in the day' when the homes were new, the lawns well-manicured, the trees leafed out, and the streets in good repair. *Children once played here*, he thought, *hopscotch, catch, and jump rope while their dads washed the family cars and their moms knitted or read on the porches.*

Now, under an overcast sky and with the air damp with mist, the neighborhood looked desolate, foreboding even, the houses stripped of paint by the elements just as the trees had been laid bare by the winds of autumn. Martelli doubted he would find grass under the soggy leaves that covered the land, not because the houses were old and in disrepair, but simply because most had no occupants to care for the grounds. Foreclosure signs, the foreign soldiers of an occupying army, stood at attention along the broken sidewalks, and few homes on the block gave indication that life could be found within.

Martelli got out of his car, and half-running, half-hopping, made his way up the sidewalk to the steps of one house. Climbing the wooden structure as quickly as he could, given his prosthetic leg, he arrived on the porch with only the slightest hint of dampness clinging to his suit coat.

Martelli had seen a light in the living room on the first floor, so he felt sure someone was home. This observation seemed to be reaffirmed by the sounds emanating from the closed window to the right of the front door . . . voices from a soap opera, if he interpreted correctly what the actors were saying.

He pushed the doorbell but heard nothing. *Hmmm . . . broken*, he thought. Moving to his right, he could not see through the curtains, but hoped whoever was home might be watching the television set he heard.

Martelli knocked on the window with the knuckle of his right forefinger. Nothing happened for a few seconds. Then, the curtains slowly parted, and a face appeared . . . the face of a woman Martelli had not seen since high school, some twenty-five years earlier. She recognized him immediately and, after motioning for him to go back to the front door, she disappeared from the window. A few seconds later he heard a chain lock being undone, followed by the release of two deadbolt locks. As the door opened, he came face to face with Vince Ponticelli's wife.

"Well, well, well. If it isn't Sergeant Louis Martelli, home from the wars." She showed no emotion, as if every ounce of energy had been drained from her body. A cigarette hung from her lips, and her eyelids drooped. Even from two feet he could smell alcohol on her breath.

"Hello, Elena. I wasn't sure you'd recognize me."

She took the cigarette out of her mouth and coughed. "I couldn't forget you, Lou, not after all the fun times we had together . . . you and Steph, Vince, and me. The days of wine and roses, as they say.

See Endnote 14.

"The Bridge" (Photo: K.S. Brooks)
Indies Unlimited, December 11, 2022[19]

**"Well, I've heard the people who own a roadhouse called Horsefeathers
south of Wrightsville on Route 624—that's over the two-lane
girder bridge other side of the Susquehanna River from Columbia—run
an illegal poker game every night but Sunday in their back room."**

---

19 Though the photo prompt is from Indies Unlimited's weekly competition
for December 11, 2022, the story was too long to submit for competition. That
said, I thank Ms. Brooks for inspiring me to present this tale.

18. The Bridge

"I'd love to find a good poker game," said NYPD Detective Louis "Lou" Martelli.

The fact is, other than his family and the NYPD, poker was Louis Martelli's life. Those trips he and his family took to Las Vegas every spring were taken in part so Martelli could spend several evenings playing five-card stud with some of the men with whom he had served in Kosovo, Kuwait, and Iraq. What was unusual about their sessions, however, was they all cheated, all the time. And they all knew it. The fun was in catching the *other* guys cheating. Martelli, however, was the master when it came to dealing from the bottom of the deck, card culling, card segregation, card assembly, and forcing errors of judgment by badgering his opponents. This is what made their Army reunions so much fun. Cheat, catch the other guys cheating, reminisce over old times, raise a bottle of beer to toast all who gave some in the war, and raise another bottle to toast those who gave all.[20]

"Well, sir, I've heard the people who own a roadhouse called Horsefeathers south of Wrightsville on Route 624—that can be reached via the new four-lane bridge over the Susquehanna River from Columbia—run an illegal poker game every night but Sunday in their back room."

Martelli was all ears. "What do you mean 'illegal poker game'?"

"Pennsylvania gaming laws, as they apply to poker, don't have charges on the books for players, only for someone who is operating a game for profit. So, the law will look the other way in cases where everyone in the game can be considered a player."

---

20 The phrase, "All gave some . . . Some gave all," was arguably first stated in a poem by the same title published in 2004 by Don Tyson. http://www.authorsden.com/visit/viewPoetry.asp?id=94475

"Okay," said Martelli. "So, what's the deal with the people at Horsefeathers?"

"They charge $50 to get into the back room and then, when they close the game down at 11 p.m., they take 30 percent of the money on the table. If the state were to find out about this, the establishment not only could be charged under the Pennsylvania gambling laws but also, could lose its liquor license."

"Sounds like Lou's kind of place," quipped Martelli's partner, NYPD Detective Sean O'Keeffe.

"Just be careful, guys. That place is frequented by an unusually rough crowd, and they don't play nice with strangers."

See Endnote 15.

"Black Hawk Down" (Photo: Pond5)

"Come on! Come on! It's going to blow!"

19. Black Hawk Down

FADE IN

INT. MARTELLI BEDROOM, EARLY MORNING (3 a.m.)
(Sound of distant thunder;
occasional lightening.
Lightening softly
illuminates two sleeping
adults. Suddenly, close
lightning strike, which
fully illuminates room,
followed instantly by
loud clap of thunder.)

SCENE CHANGES TO
CENTRAL IRAQ

SUB-TITLE: CENTRAL IRAQ, APRIL 2, 2003

INT. DOWNED BLACK HAWK

Burning Black Hawk; rounds going off; blinding flashes of
light; audible alarm (klaxon-like); figure in cargo doorway
is crew chief, MARTELLI. Flames everywhere. MARTELLI
motions to PILOTS to get out.

MARTELLI

Come on! Come on! It's going to
blow!

PILOT (O.S.)
(Screaming)
Can't move! Get out! That's an

order!

                    PILOT, CO-PILOT (O.S.)
                    (Screaming)

Martelli moves towards cockpit to save pilots when explosion
throws him back towards cargo door, shattering his left leg
and almost incapacitating him. He struggles to his feet and
tries to move forward again, only to be blown out cargo door
by another blast.

CLOSE-UP OF MARTELLI'S FACE; PAINED, DIRTY, GREASY,
SWEATY

                                    FADE TO BLACK.
                                    KLAXON-LIKE
                                    SOUND MORPHS TO
                                    VIBRATING,
                                    BUZZING
                                    CELLPHONE ON
                                    HIS BEDSTAND

INT. BEDROOM, EARLY MORNING (3:10 a.m.)

Lightening illuminates Martelli's face in same pose as on the
battlefield. He gropes for cellphone, finds it, and opens
line.

                    MARTELLI
                    (Martelli had been the
                    crew member aboard a
                    Black Hawk helicopter
                    that was shot down in the
                    April, 2003, invasion of
                    Baghdad during Operation
                    Iraqi Freedom. Now, with
                    the help of a prosthetic
                    leg, he walked with a
                    slight limp. He worked
                    for NYPD under a special

waiver issued by the
mayor.)
Martelli!

CENTRAL DISPATCH (V.O.; COMING
FROM CELLPHONE)
Get down to the Financial District.
ANTONETTI will meet you there...at
The Bowling Green Bull!

MARTELLI
I'm on it.

Terminates call. Places cellphone on bedstand. Opens drawer.
Lightening illuminates service revolver in shoulder holster
and badge, and prosthetic leg resting against bedstand. Hand
from woman next to him touches his right shoulder.

STEPHANIE
Is everything okay? Are *you* okay?

MARTELLI
I'm fine, Steph. Something's come
up. I'll call you later.

Places his left hand on top of hers, pats it twice, gets up,
and hops to the bathroom with his service revolver, badge,
and prosthetic leg.

AERIAL SHOT OF
UNMARKED PATROL
CAR WITH
FLASHING, RED,
DASHBOARD-
MOUNTED BEACON
HEADING OUT OF
BROOKLYN INTO
MANHATTAN AND
TOWARDS THE
FINANCIAL

101

DISTRICT.
LIGHTENING IN
THE DISTANCE
(STORM ABATING).

See Endnote 16.

"Marshmallows" (Photo: K.S. Brooks)
Indies Unlimited, December 18, 2022

**"We all pitched in with the plowing, planting,
and harvesting of the wheat . . ."**

21. Marshmallows

"We divorced six years ago," she said, with a tinge of regret in her voice. "I still love him, and we have a very good relationship. He has custody of our son, Connor. Still, the boy always comes over to my apartment when I'm in town. My former husband and I even go out to dinner and a movie at times, and I'm very much engaged in our Connor's education, as is my 'ex'. Plus, we share the cost of Connor's upbringing equally. I know it sounds strange, but it works.

"I sometimes wish things had turned out differently. I was brought up in the Midwest, on a farm outside the little town of Bigfork, Minnesota. You've probably never heard of it. It's just to the northeast of the Chippewa National Forest. Family was, and still is, everything."

"Amen to that," said NYPD Detective Louis "Lou" Martelli.

"I had three older brothers," she continued. "We all pitched in with the plowing, planting, and harvesting of the wheat; slopping the pigs; milking the cows; birthing calves . . . you name it, we did it."

"Sounds idyllic," said Martelli, half joking.

"Oh, yeah. My favorite was helping Dad treat cows when they came down with milk fever," she said facetiously. "But seriously, if something broke, we were the ones who had to fix it. I remember when I was 16 helping Dad rebuild the engine on our old John Deere 2840 utility tractor. Now *that* was a dirty job!"

See Endnote 17.

"Last Respects" (Photo" New Africa, Big Stock Photo)

"The guy's been dead for days."

22. Last Rites

New York Police Detective Louis Martelli pulled his unmarked *Crown Vic* to the curb in front of the Church of the Holy Redeemer in Lower Manhattan, blocking the funeral procession's lead vehicle and further heightening the tension among the people on the sidewalk. The funeral director, family, and mourners, puzzled by the unusual turn of events, stood there, conversing quietly. Occasionally, someone glanced nervously at the church's entrance. None, however, was allowed back into the building. Two police officers moved among them, rapidly gathering names and other information in preparation for handing their notes to the lead detective—Martelli—for follow-up.

Martelli lifted his left leg over the driver-side door threshold, something necessitated by an old Iraqi War injury. Once out of his car, he made his way up the steps and into the sanctuary. Walking hurriedly toward the altar, he stopped briefly at a point halfway down the aisle, steadied himself on a pew, genuflected, and made the Sign of the Cross before proceeding to the casket.

"Well, well, well, if it ain't Mrs. Martelli's *wunderkind*, Master Sergeant Louis Martelli . . . war hero, Master Detective, and all-about-town *bon vivant!* The last time I saw you and Antonetti together you were chasing the Headless Horseman in Central Park. Remember? It was the case of the serial killer who sliced and diced that pharmaceutical executive behind the Delacourt Theater."

Crime scene investigator Robin Peterson loved to spar with Martelli. A flirt who wore her flaming red hair long, stringy, and parted in the middle, she never let an opportunity go by to tease him.

"People at headquarters are still wondering about you two," she chortled, referring to Martelli and Deputy Coroner Michael Antonetti, who was examining the embalmed remains of an elderly man lying in a coffin to the front of the altar. "Are you two a couple, or aren't you? That's the $64,000 question."

Martelli laughed. "Peterson, are you still knifing guys in the back on Saturday nights, so you'll get called to crime scenes and have something to do other than sit at home watching old movies? I mean, when was the last time you had a date?"

Antonetti scowled. "Come on, you two, have a little respect for the dead. This is a holy place of worship!" He was in the last stages of examining the remains in a coffin that was mounted on a mobile display cart.

Peterson resumed her work, taking pictures of the area around the casket and looking for evidence on the floor around it.

Martelli approached Antonetti. "Pardon me for asking, Michael, but what are we doing here? Obviously, the deceased is dead, he's been embalmed, and this was a funeral service intended to send him on his way to the Great Beyond. Yet, here we are, some of New York's Finest . . . one of New York City's most skilled deputy coroners, the best CSI in the business—he winked at Peterson—and Manhattan's top Detective-Investigator. You would think someone's been shot!"

"He was."

"Who?"

"The deceased."

"You gotta to be kidding! When?"

"Based on what I was told, sometime in the last hour or so."

"Come on, Antonetti. The guy's been dead for days."

"I didn't say he was alive when he was shot."

"This isn't another one of your pranks, is it?"

"Nope. I may have pulled a few mischievous tricks in my day—"

"'Mischievous tricks?' Is that what you call them? Like the time you put a fake severed hand covered with blood in my car's trunk—"

Antonetti waved him off. "A childish prank to be sure, Louis. But this is the real thing. The man's been shot . . . the bullet was fired at close range, right through the casket, by someone who apparently came to pay their respects."

"Well, they sure had a strange way of doing it.

"Who discovered the bullet hole?"

"The funeral director, just as he was closing the casket in preparation for moving it to the hearse. That's when he asked everyone to step outside and wait while he called the police."

"And nobody heard anything?"

Peterson looked up. "Before you ask, Martelli, I already grabbed, bagged, and marked as evidence the video tapes from the church's surveillance system. Maybe Missy Dugan will be able to figure out what happened."

"Thanks, Red.

"Anything else you can tell me, Michael?"

"I may be able to say more once I get the corpse back to the morgue. But there is one more thing you should know. It has to do with something I never expected to find."

"What's that?"

"Someone, probably the shooter, stuffed a piece of garlic into the corpse's mouth."

"Garlic?"

"Yes. It's an old Romanian ritual used to ensure a vampire doesn't rise from the dead."

"Oh, that's just great! The next thing you're gonna tell me is that the slug is made of silver!"

"Those generally are used to kill werewolves, Louis, but I guess they'd work on vampires as well."

See Endnote 18.

"Glitter" (Photo: K.S. Brooks)
Indies Unlimited, December 25, 2022

"The only outside decorations you and Marcy put out
during the holidays are those five ornaments,
the string of lights, and some glitter . . . "

23. Glitter

"**F**rank, Merry Christmas to you and Judy."
"Same to you and Marcy, Jeff. Hope the New Year brings you and the family good health and happiness."

"Thanks, and the same to you and yours. By the way, I've been meaning to ask you—and I hope you don't mind—"

"No, go ahead."

"Well, as you know, we're new to the block. Marcy and I couldn't help noticing since we moved here 2 years ago, the only outside decorations you and Judy put out during the holidays are those five ornaments, the string of lights, and some glitter on that evergreen at the corner of your house. Is there a reason for that?"

[Frank chuckled] "Actually, that tree was planted back in the late 1980s as a high school project by our son, Jimmy. The ornaments and lights are some of the decorations we had at that time, though they were used to decorate the tree in our living room. Judy found them in the attic a few years ago. We thought it would be a nice tribute to Jimmy if we hung them on 'his' tree every year at this time in his memory."

"In his memory?" What happened to him?"

"His UH-60 Black Hawk helicopter crashed on April 2nd, 2003. He was the first West Point graduate to die in Iraq."

See Endnote 19.

■ *Theodore Jerome Cohen*

Endnotes

1. The Doves Type

⁋ THE DOVES TYPE® is Robert Green's digital recreation of the Doves Press Fount of Type.

Original type conceived, commissioned & directed by T. J. Cobden-Sanderson, London, 1899.

Developed by Emery Walker, assisted by Percy Tiffin, at Walker & Boutall, London, 1899 — 1900.

Punches cut by Edward Prince, London, 1899 — 1901.

Produced in a single size, 2 Line Brevier (16 pt), by Miller & Richard, Edinburgh, 1899 — 1905.

First sorts delivered October 1899, full fount of characters completed July 1901.

Punches & matrices thrown into the River Thames by T. J. Cobden-Sanderson, March 1913.

Entire type dropped into the River Thames by T. J. Cobden-Sanderson, August 1916 — January 1917.

Digital facsimile Doves Type® developed 2010 — 2015.

OpenType Version 1.0 released December 2013. Version 2.0 released January 2015.

Created using sources from original Doves Press publications & 150 metal sorts recovered from the River Thames by Robert Green & the Port of London Authority salvage team, October & November 2014.

The Doves Type® — www.dovestype.com

Distributed by Typespec Ltd — www.typespec.co.uk

2. Stakeout

This story is adapted from Ted's novel *House of Cards: Dead Men Tell No Tales*. This is the second book in the Detective Louis Martelli, NYPD, mystery/thriller series of six books. The novels may be read in any order. The books can be found in eBook, paperback, hardcover, and audiobook formats at Amazon, B&N, Kobo, and other booksellers worldwide.

https://www.amazon.com/gp/product/B07J2XFRVP/?ie=UTF8&%2AVersion%2A=1&%2Aentries%2A=0

3. Wheel of Fortune

This story is adapted from Ted's mystery/thriller *Wheel of Fortune*, the sixth book in the Detective Louis Martelli, NYPD, series. You can find more information about this book (and series) at:

https://www.amazon.com/gp/product/B07J2XFRVP/?ie=UTF8&%2AVersion%2A=1&%2Aentries%2A=0

4. Accidentally, On Purpose, Dead

This story, based on facts, was excerpted from, and modified after, Ted's sixth novel in his NYPD Detective Louis Martelli, NYPD, Mystery/Thriller Series, *Wheel of Fortune*. For more information on this book, see:

https://www.theodore-cohen-novels.com/wheeloffortune.html

The book is available in Kindle, paperback, and audiobook editions from Amazon:

https://www.amazon.com/dp/B00TNEDSBC

As well, it can be found on B&N in paperback and Nook, and on Kobo:

https://www.barnesandnoble.com/w/wheel-of-fortune-theodore-jerome-cohen/1121225387?ean=9780984920969 https://www.kobo.com/us/en/ebook/wheel-of-fortune-11

Books in this series can be read in any order.

5 506
This story, based on facts, was excerpted from, and modified after, Ted's fourth novel in his NYPD Detective Louis Martelli, NYPD, Mystery/Thriller Series, *Night Shadows*. For more information on this book, see:

https://www.theodore-cohen-novels.com/nightshadows.html

The book is available in Kindle, paperback, and audiobook editions from Amazon:

https://www.amazon.com/dp/B00J828Q20

As well, it can be found on B&N in paperback and Nook, and on Kobo:

https://www.barnesandnoble.com/w/night-shadows-theodore-cohen/1118958347?ean=9780984920983

https://www.kobo.com/us/en/ebook/night-shadows-15

Books in this series can be read in any order.

6. Porch
This is an excerpt from Ted's mystery thriller, *Lilith: Demon in the Night*. A modern-day vampire story. You can learn more about his novel at:

https://www.theodore-cohen-novels.com/lilith.html

The book is available in the Kindle, paperback, and audiobook formats from Amazon:

https://www.amazon.com/Lilith-Demon-Homicide-Detective-Martelli-ebook/dp/B006ZZDQNC

It also is available from B&N and Kobo.

7. Missing

NYPD Homicide Detectives Louis "Lou" Martelli and Sean O'Keeffe are featured in Ted's six-book mystery/thriller series available on Amazon.com and through other online retail outlets. Information on the six novels, which can be read in any order, may be found here:

https://www.theodore-cohen-novels.com/

On Amazon.com, the six books are found here:

https://tinyurl.com/yxyr3sph

The award-winning novels are available from Amazon.com in the Kindle, paperback, and audiobook formats.

8. Magic

This short story comprises three excerpts from Ted's mystery/thriller *Lilith: Demon of the Night*, a modern-day vampire novel. You can read more about the story at:

https://www.theodore-cohen-novels.com/lilith.html

The book is available on Amazon in Kindle, paperback, and audiobook:

https://www.amazon.com/Lilith-Demon-Homicide-Detective-Martelli-ebook/dp/B006ZZDQNC

It also is available from B&N and Kobo.

The six books in the Martelli mystery/thriller series can be read in any order.

Here is the flash fiction tale (249 words) actually submitted for the photographic prompt posted on Indies Unlimited for August 7, 2021:

"Magic" (Photo: K.S. Brooks)
Indies Unlimited, August 7, 2021

Truth be told, Stephanie Martelli would have loved to see her husband's partner, NYPD Homicide Detective Sean O'Keeffe, find a lovely woman and settle down. For now, that didn't seem to be in the cards. True, Sean never was at a loss for finding women to date. He always showed up at the precinct Christmas parties and other celebrations with a beautiful lady on his arm, *but never the same one twice.* There was no reason to suspect the woman with whom he had been dancing the previous evening would fare better than Sean's previous *amores.*

After Lou, Stephanie's husband, finished speaking with her on the phone, he dressed, packed and stowed his suitcase in the trunk of their precinct's *Crown Vic,* and walked to Sean's motel room.

O'Keeffe, dripping wet with a bath towel wrapped around his waist, let Martelli in. He had a smile on his face.

"Lou, we had the most fantastic time. What a terrific dancer she is! It was magic. We danced on the terrace and watched the Moon set over the lake, turning the waves near the shore electric blue. If it wasn't for the fact she had to get up at 5:30, get her daughter to school, and do rounds at the hospital, we would've danced all night."

Lou smiled. "I'm really happy for you, Sean." What he was thinking was: *You're a goner, Sean. If I were you, I'd see a priest as soon as possible to receive your last rites.*

9. The City Below

Ted thought his readers might enjoy this prompt-appropriate excerpt from a screenplay he wrote based on his novel *Death by Wall Street: Rampage of the Bulls*. The screenplay was edited by Hollywood screenwriter and editor Howard Allen ("the Script Doctor) and was entered into the 2012 Zoetrope Screenplay Competition sponsored by Francis Ford Coppola. Alas, it was not selected for a prize. Additional information on the screenplay can be found here:

https://www.theodore-cohen-novels.com/dbws-screenplay.html

The screenplay was published in paperback; it may be found here:

https://www.amazon.com/gp/product/B09RLQNMDV

The character of Homicide Detective Louis Martelli, NYPD, is based on the life and death of Ted's friend, Army Captain and pilot James F. "Jimmy" Adamouski. Ted's novel, *Eighth Circle: A Special Place in Hell*, is dedicated to Jimmy. Jimmy, who was to enter Harvard Business School in the fall of 2003, was killed in action when his Black Hawk helicopter crashed in central Iraq on April 2, 2003, during Operation Iraqi Freedom. His remains were buried with full military honors in both Arlington National Cemetery and West Point Cemetery. You can learn more about Jimmy in the Afterword of this novel:

https://www.theodore-cohen-novels.com/eighthcircle.html

10. Progress

This is an excerpt from Ted's mystery/thriller, *Eighth Circle: A Special Place in Hell*. This is the 5th book in the Detective Louis Martelli, NYPD, Mystery/Thriller Series. The books may be read in any order. On Amazon, the novel is available for Kindle as well as in paperback and audiobook formats:

https://www.amazon.com/Eighth-Circle-Detective-Martelli-Thriller-ebook/dp/B00PG5QM1K

11. Shackleford's Lament

This is an excerpt from Ted's mystery/thriller, *Eighth Circle: A Special Place in Hell*. This is the 5th book in the Detective Louis Martelli, NYPD, Mystery/Thriller Series. The books may be read in any order. On Amazon, the novel is available for Kindle as well as in paperback and audiobook formats:

https://www.amazon.com/Eighth-Circle-Detective-Martelli-Thriller-ebook/dp/B00PG5QM1K

12. Lunch

This story is a modified excerpt from Ted's mystery/thriller on modern-day vampirism, *Lilith: Demon of the Night*. The novel can be found on Amazon and other online booksellers' websites.

https://www.theodore-cohen-novels.com/lilith.html

https://www.amazon.com/Lilith-Demon-Homicide-Detective-Martelli-ebook/dp/B006ZZDQNC

13. Need for Speed

This story is a modified excerpt from Ted's mystery/thriller on modern-day vampirism, *Lilith: Demon of the Night*. The novel can be found on Amazon and other online booksellers' websites.

https://www.theodore-cohen-novels.com/lilith.html

https://www.amazon.com/Lilith-Demon-Homicide-Detective-Martelli-ebook/dp/B006ZZDQNC

14. Disrepair

This story is an excerpt from Ted's mystery/thriller *House of Cards: Dead Men Tell No Tales*. The novel can be found on Amazon and other online booksellers' websites.

https://www.theodore-cohen-novels.com/houseofcards2.html

https://www.amazon.com/dp/B09B9QTTQZ

15. The Bridge

This story is a modified excerpt from Ted's mystery/thriller on the mob's efforts to take over the trash hauling and recycling business in Lancaster and York, PA, *Wheel of Fortune*. The novel can be found on Amazon and other online booksellers' websites.

https://www.theodore-cohen-novels.com/wheeloffortune.html

https://www.amazon.com/dp/B00TNEDSBC

16. Black Hawk Down

This is the first scene of Ted's screenplay *Death by Wall Street*, which was adapted from Ted's novel by the same title. The screenplay can be obtained in paperback format from Amazon:

https://www.theodore-cohen-novels.com/dbws-screenplay.html

https://www.amazon.com/gp/product/B09RLQNMDV

The story is based on real events that occurred during the development, and the (alleged) corrupt review by the US Food and Drug Administration (FDA) in 2007, of a revolutionary new treatment for prostate cancer. (In the novel and screenplay, the disease discussed is breast cancer.) The impediments faced by the drug development company in bringing their product to market, erected both by the FDA and Wall Street, were and are as described by Ted. Lending credence to Ted's assertions the FDA's review committee was corrupted by certain of its members is the fact Ted was asked to come to New York City in October, 2012, and brief the FBI. While the Bureau found his evidence compelling, the statute of limitations had, unfortunately, run out on the crimes Ted alleged certain doctors on the FDA staff and on the advisory committee had committed.

17. Marshmallows

This story is a modified excerpt from Ted's mystery/thriller on the mob's efforts to take over the trash hauling and recycling business in Lancaster and York, PA, *Wheel of Fortune*. The novel can be found on Amazon and other online booksellers' websites.

https://www.theodore-cohen-novels.com/wheeloffortune.html

https://www.amazon.com/dp/B00TNEDSBC

18. Last Rites

This story is a modified excerpt from Ted's mystery/thriller on modern-day vampirism, *Lilith: Demon of the Night*. The novel can be found on Amazon and other online booksellers' websites.

https://www.theodore-cohen-novels.com/lilith.html

https://www.amazon.com/Lilith-Demon-Homicide-Detective-Martelli-ebook/dp/B006ZZDQNC

19. Glitter

"Jimmy" was James Francis Adamouski, CPT, United States Army, a friend of Ted's and his wife Susan, and son of their good friends, Judy and LTC Frank Adamouski, US Army (ret.). Frank and Ted worked together for many years, traveling occasionally from Washington, DC, to Ft. Monmouth, NJ, for their work. When in New Jersey, they took time and headed north to visit Jimmy, who was a cadet at the United States Military Academy at West Point, NY. There, he not only excelled academically but in sports as well, soccer being his game of choice. Ted and Frank had many a good meal together at The Thayer Hotel. And what an honor it was for those who attended Jimmy and Meighan's wedding in Savannah, Georgia, after his graduation, to witness the solemn ceremony with its military formality and to attend the beautiful reception that followed.

Upon graduation, Jimmy attended flight school at Ft. Rutger, Alabama, where he learned to fly Black Hawk helicopters. His first overseas deployment was in support of the US efforts to quell the Kosovo conflict, where, as a lay Eucharist minister in the Catholic Church, the troops took to calling him "Father Jimmy" because he conducted prayer services for his fellow soldiers. Jimmy, who was to enter Harvard Business School in the fall of 2003, was killed in action when his Black Hawk helicopter crashed in central Iraq on April 2, 2003, during Operation Iraqi Freedom. His remains were buried with full military honors in Arlington National Cemetery and West Point Cemetery.

If someone were to conclude Jimmy was the inspiration for the character Louis Martelli in Ted's NYPD mystery/thriller novels, they would be correct.

Rest in peace, Jimmy. Thank you for your service to our country.

**Photo courtesy of the Adamouski Family: Judy, Frank, Karen, Laura,
Jaclyn, and Meighan (Jimmy's wife)**

James Francis Adamouski, Captain, United States Army
2nd Battalion, 3rd Aviation Regiment, Hunter Army Airfield, Georgia
Died in Central Iraq, April 2, 2003, at the age of 29.

■ *Theodore Jerome Cohen*

The Six Det. Louis "Lou" Martelli, NYPD, Mystery/Thriller Novels

NB: Books may be read in any order.

https://www.amazon.com/gp/product/B07HRFJ8 FT/ref=series_rw_dp_sw

1. *Death by Wall Street: Rampage of the Bulls* (Detective Louis Martelli, NYPD, Mystery/Thriller Series Book 1)

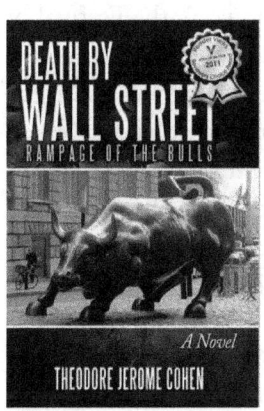

Death by Wall Street: Rampage of the Bulls, a murder mystery, is based on real events. It is the story of how the oligarchs of Wall Street, doctors and others in the pharmaceutical research profession having significant conflicts of interest, and employees of two 'captured' US government agencies the Securities and Exchange Commission (SEC) and the Food and Drug Administration (FDA) by design as well as by simply refusing to pursue the evidence of malfeasance provided to them, deny patients lifesaving treatments that are demonstrated safe and effective in FDA-approved drug trials. When the severed head of a Wall Street stock analyst turns up spiked on a horn of the Wall Street Bull, Detective Louis Martelli of the NYPD is assigned to track down the murderer. But why were this victim and the victims of two similar murders that followed singled out for execution? Martelli eventually learns the answer to this question and tracks down the killer, but not before uncovering some of Wall Street's and the US government's darkest secrets pertaining to the US financial markets and the nation's health care practices. For a video trailer, see: http://www.youtube.com/watch?v=kIbhmPCckpQ

2. *House Of Cards: Dead Men Tell No Tales* (Detective Louis Martelli, NYPD, Mystery/Thriller Series Book 2)

Who Killed Matthew B. Richardson III?

Banksters or Islamic Terrorists?

"Cohen's style is not unlike that found in novels by authors such as Dan Brown, or Tom Clancy, or even the late Michael Crichton." Gary Sorkin for Pacific Book Review. The head of one of the largest investment banking and securities firms in the United States has been assassinated on Times Square in the middle of New York City's annual celebration of Halloween, the Festival of the Dead. Louis Martelli, NYPD, is one of the first detectives on the scene. The case rapidly spirals downward into a maelstrom of death and intrigue linked both to the financial meltdown of 2008 and international terrorism. Who is behind the murders, and why is the FBI attempting to shutdown Martelli's investigation before it even can get started? Martelli eventually learns the answers to these and other questions, but not before discovering how two Wall Street financial institutions have been complicit in funding Islamic terrorism. (Adult language)

3. **Lilith...Demon of the Night** (Detective Louis Martelli, NYPD, Mystery/Thriller Series Book 3)

When a man walks into a Catholic church just prior to the start of a funeral service, stuffs garlic into the deceased's mouth and pumps a bullet into the corpse, NYPD Homicide Detective Louis Martelli is as puzzled as he's ever been on a case. No stranger to the macabre, Martelli is even more mystified by Deputy Coroner Michael Antonetti's findings, which confirm that the deceased, far from having died of respiratory failure and a possible heart attack, was murdered by someone who injected him with a lethal dose of Philippine Cobra venom. When other, similar deaths are uncovered in and around New York City, the investigation conducted by Martelli and his partner, Detective Sean O'Keeffe, takes a decidedly morbid turn, leading to the discovery of a modern-day vampire cult, a woman named 'Lilith,' and a serial killer with a score to settle. Who is behind the killings, and can Martelli and O'Keeffe stop him before he kills his last victim and makes good his escape? The answers to these and other questions will be found in this gripping, modern-day tale of vampirism unlike any you have read.

4. **Night Shadows** (Detective Louis Martelli, NYPD, Mystery/Thriller Series Book 4)

When a wealthy Wall Street commodity futures trader is found dead in his townhouse of an apparent drug overdose, Deputy Coroner Michael Antonetti, NYPD, is suspicious. Antonetti tells Detective Louis Martelli he suspects what appears to be a suicide may in fact be murder. After a similar case is discovered involving a former friend of the Wall Street trader who played on the same high school football team almost twenty years earlier, Martelli is convinced he is dealing with someone bent on revenge. But the two teammates who ostensibly committed suicide were part of an elite three-man squad known as The Flying Horsemen. This convinces Martelli there will be a third victim. But who might it be, and could the killings have anything to do with the rape and suicide of some of the men's former high school classmates? The answers will be found in this mystery/thriller that will keep you on the edge of your seat until the very end.

5. *Eighth Circle: A Special Place in Hell* (Detective Louis Martelli, NYPD, Mystery/Thriller Series Book 5)

When the mayor of New York City's grandson and the grandson's wife are murdered execution-style in their Tribeca apartment, NYPD Detective Louis Martelli and his partner, Detective Sean O'Keeffe, are left completely in the dark. Months go by without any actionable leads until a meeting with the wife's doctor and the bizarre torching of Stephanie Martelli's car turn the investigation upside down and land Martelli and O'Keeffe in the hotseat. When an old friend of Pietro Martelli's, Louis's deceased father and a former street cop who had been gunned down in the line of duty, sends Martelli a note asking for a meeting, thing stake an even stranger turn. The evidence in this mob-driven case of political corruption, bribery, and murder pits the two detectives against their boss, Captain Hanlon, Police Commissioner Eugene Fields, and His Honor the Mayor. Can Martelli and O'Keeffe survive this kind of pressure and keep their jobs, much less solve the case? You'll have to read Eighth Circle to learn the answers.

6. *Wheel of Fortune* (Detective Louis Martelli, NYPD, Mystery/Thriller Series Book 6)

WHEEL OF FORTUNE

THEODORE JEROME COHEN

A DETECTIVE LOUIS MARTELLI, NYPD, MYSTERY/THRILLER

Even as a child, Katlyn Lundquist was drop-dead gorgeous. She also was willful. In her teens, perhaps out of spite, she created her own name and persona. As she grew up, she readily accepted money and gifts from her parents but thumbed her nose at society in general and her parent's way of life in particular. A seeming infatuation with Tommie Lupinacci, head of a major crime-infested cartage association based in Brooklyn, led her to move east with the mobster. But when she showed up dead with a bullet in the back of her head, NYPD Detectives Louis Martelli and Sean O'Keeffe were stumped. If this were a mob hit, why dump her body in plain sight? Moreover, who was she and what was the motive for killing her? The investigation leads to the area around Lundquist's hometown in eastern Pennsylvania and to the mob's efforts to take over the trash hauling and recycling business in Lancaster and York, PA. It's only after Martelli brings IT Specialist Missy Dugan into the case that he and O'Keeffe are able to unravel the mystery.

■ *Theodore Jerome Cohen*

Two Det. Louis "Lou" Martelli, NYPD, Mystery/Thriller Screenplays

1. Death by Wall Street: Rampage of the Bulls

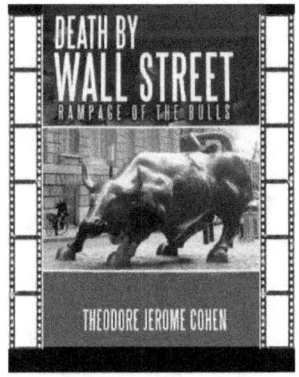

When the severed head of a Wall Street stock analyst turns up spiked on a horn of the Wall Street Bull, Detective Louis Martelli of the NYPD is assigned to track down the murderer. But why were this victim and the victims of two similar murders that followed singled out for execution? Martelli eventually learns the answer to this question and tracks down the killer, but not before uncovering some of Wall Street's and the US government's darkest secrets pertaining to the US financial markets and the nation's health care practices.

https://www.amazon.com/gp/product/Bo9RLQNMDV

2. Beware Those Closest (based on House of Cards)

When the head of the sixth largest investment banking and securities firm in the United States is assassinated on Times Square in the middle of New York City's annual Festival of the Dead, Homicide Detective Louis Martelli is one of the first on the scene. Working quickly, NYPD Information Specialist Missy Dugan quickly identifies the assassin, but the case rapidly spirals downward into a maelstrom of death and international intrigue linked both to the financial meltdown of 2008 and Islamic terrorism. Who was behind the murders, and why did the Federal Bureau of Investigation (FBI) attempt to shut down Martelli's investigation before he was even able to begin work in earnest? Martelli eventually learns the answers to these and other questions as he tracks down the killer, but not before uncovering some of Wall Street's darkest secrets, including a plot to fund terrorism from within the depths of the Street's financial institutions.

https://www.amazon.com/gp/product/B09RM5XDKK

Characters

Death by Wall Street: Rampage of the Bulls
Key Characters

1. Louis Fiorello Martelli, Homicide Detective, NYPD. Disabled Iraqi War veteran. Wears prosthesis on left leg as a result of a helicopter crash that occurred during the invasion of Baghdad in 2003. Serves on the Force under a waiver from the Mayor of New York City. Cool, cocky, flippant. Card shark *extraordinaire*. Good Samaritan.

2. Stephanie Martelli, Louis's wife. Wears velvet gloves on steel gauntlets. Literally saved husband's life after he was discharged a broken man. Manages an HVAC firm in Brooklyn.

3. Missy Dugan, Senior IT Specialist, NYPD. Has forgotten more than Bill Gates ever knew. Martelli's 'go to' person for things technical. A pixie. Has a 'mouth.' Maniacal laugh.

4. Alexa Lindsay Beauvais, Senior Financial Forensic Specialist, NYPD. Brilliant Wharton MBA. Knows her way around Wall Street and Washington. In her 30s. Tall, statuesque. Lives with her mother, who suffers from Alzheimer's.

5. John Williamson, Senior Stock Analyst, Bartlett, Cline, and Stephenson. High roller. Has a $5 million condo on the Upper West Side. Mocks the 'Little People.'

6. Steve Jacobs, Mid-Level Stock Analyst, Bartlett, Cline, and Stephenson. Williamson's assistant. Family man, decent guy.

7. Tricia Fournier (aka The Dragon Lady). Executive Vice President and Manager, Equities Research, Bartlett, Cline, and Stephenson. First Class Bitch. Demetri Mihailov's lover.

8. Dr. Paul Broussard, Consultant to, and Special Government Employee of, the FDA. Bought and paid for by the pharmaceutical industry.

9. Demetri Mihailov, MD, President, CEO, and Chairman of the Board, BCaPharmaceutical Corporation. Never heard of the Hippocratic Oath.

10. Selma Holtzmann, Farmer, Orange County, NY. Dying from HER2-positive breast cancer.
11. Terrell Holtzmann, Farmer, Orange County, NY. Selma's son.
12. Brad Hutchinson, Sheriff, Orange County, NY. From the old school. Never shot a man in his life.
13. Millie Ferguson, Reporter, *Goshen* (NY) *Sentinel-Courier*. Selma Holtzmann's stepdaughter from her second marriage. Looks younger than her age. Tough. Could pick your brain clean, and you wouldn't know it.
14. Sergeant Luke Sanders, Charlie Company, 1st Battalion, 20th Infantry Regiment, 11th Brigade, 23rd Infantry Division. US Army Viet Nam veteran. Tried to stop the 1968 My Lai Massacre.
15. Edward Cunningham, Master Butcher. Selma Holtzmann's foster child. Brilliant, well read. Dealt a bad hand in life.

Supporting characters:

1. Rob and Tiffany Martelli. The Martelli's teenage children.
2. Homicide Detective Sean O'Keeffe, Martelli's partner. Ex-MP. Iraqi War veteran.
3. Homicide Detectives Eddy Lewis and Mary Fitzpatrick, Martelli's co-workers of at the First Precinct. Bulldogs.
4. Michael Antonetti, MD, Deputy Coroner, NYPD. Great sense of humor, even under the grimmest circumstances.
5. Homicide Detective Jamar Jackson, Washington DC Police Department.
6. Robin (Red) Peterson, NYPD Crime Scene Investigator. Knows her stuff. A tease.
7. Tim Miles, IT Manager, Bartlett, Cline, and Stephenson.
8. Sam Conover, Esq., Corporate Lawyer for Bartlett, Cline, and Stephenson.
9. Anthony DeCarlo, Member of the Board of Directors, BCaPharmaceutical Corporation. Thorn in Mihailov's side.
10. Timothy Hanlon, Captain, First Precinct, NYPD. Martelli's supervisor. Tough, no-nonsense guy who watches out for Number One.

Beware Those Closest

Key characters:

1. Louis Fiorello Martelli, Homicide Detective, NYPD. Disabled Iraqi War veteran. Wears prosthesis on left leg as a result of a helicopter crash that occurred during the invasion of Baghdad in 2003. Serves on the Force under a waiver from the Mayor of New York City. Cool, cocky, flippant. Card shark *extraordinaire*. Good Samaritan.

2. Stephanie Martelli, Louis's wife. Wears velvet gloves on steel gauntlets. Literally saved husband's life after he was discharged a 'broken man.' Manages an HVAC firm in Brooklyn.

3. Matthew B. Richardson III, President, Chief Executive Officer, and Chairman of the Board, Richardson Stanfield & Cooper, one of the largest investment banking and securities firm in the United States. In his 50s. Estelle, his first wife of 30 years, passed away from ovarian cancer after a short but painful battle with the disease. Now married to the former Collette Marceaux of Paris, with whom he is madly in love.

4. Collette Richardson, second wife of Matthew Richardson, a woman of medium height whose short, blonde hair contains platinum highlights, is 10 years younger than him. She is madly in love with Matthew.

5. Viktor Kuznetsov, Russian assassin who dressed as a pirate.

6. Vince Ponticelli, Louis Martelli's boyhood friend from Brooklyn. Works for Yasuji. The cab driver who picks up Kuznetsov after he murders Richardson.

7. Missy Dugan, Senior IT Specialist, NYPD. Has forgotten more than Bill Gates ever knew. Martelli's 'go to' person for things technical. A pixie. Has a 'mouth.' Maniacal laugh.

8. Alexa Lindsay Beauvais, Senior Financial Forensic Specialist, NYPD. Brilliant Wharton MBA. Knows her way around Wall Street and Washington. In her 30s. Tall, statuesque. Lives with her mother, who suffers from Alzheimer's.

9. Homicide Detective Sean O'Keeffe, Martelli's partner. Ex-MP. Iraqi War vet.

10. Homicide Detectives Eddy Lewis and Mary Fitzpatrick, Martelli's co-workers of at the First Precinct.
11. Michael Antonetti, MD, Deputy Coroner, NYPD. Great sense of humor, even under the grimmest circumstances.
12. Timothy Hanlon, Captain, First Precinct, NYPD. Martelli's supervisor. Tough, no-nonsense. Watches out for Number One.
13. Ron Bishop, Special Agent in Charge, New York Field Office, Federal Bureau of Investigation (FBI)
14. Sanjar Shahrestani, President, Shahrestani & Associates, one of the most successful hedge funds on Wall Street. In his late 40s. Born in Baghdad, raised in Paris, educated in London and Boston. Richardson's best friend.
15. Mansoor Yasuji, a member of the Iranian Revolutionary Guards. In the US 20 years masquerading as a businessman. Swarthy, mustachioed, menacing. 'Owns' Shahrestani.
16. Brian Aronson, employee of Shahrestani & Associates. MBA from Stanford. Specialized in mortgage-backed securities.
17. Elena Ponticelli, Vince's wife. Stephanie's and Louis's good friend from high school.

Supporting characters:

1. Rob and Tiffany Martelli. The Martelli's teenage children.
2. Man dressed as 'Gary Grant' for a Halloween party in SoHo.
3. Dan Wilson, bartender at bar into which pirate runs after killing Richardson.
4. Ed McGuire, bar owner. In his 40s, short, bald, grossly overweight.
5. John Shackelford, Parole Officer, NYPD. Fifty years old. Short, slight of build, and wears bifocals. A walking nicotine stain.
6. Jimmy 'The Mole' Esposito. Small-time Mafioso hood. Former member of the Bianchi family. Has a cancerous mole on his right cheek.
7. Ben Jacobson, manager of Esposito's apartment building in Manhattan's Little Italy. Short, rotund man with a thin mustache.
8. Pauline, Collette's maid.
9. Sholeh Alizadeh, Sanjar Shahrestani's Executive Assistant.

10. Juliana, waitress at a restaurant in the Time Warner Building, Manhattan.
11. Ned Patterson, employee of Shahrestani & Associates
12. Teymour Kazemi, aka The Fat Man. Yasuji's 'enforcer.' Carries an Uzi and a concealed pistol behind his back.

■ *Theodore Jerome Cohen*

About the Author

Theodore Jerome "Ted" Cohen is an award-winning author who has published more than ten novels—all but one of them mystery/thrillers—as well as two books of short stories and twenty flash fiction anthologies. His *Mementos* anthologies of short-story and flash-fiction comprises a series of six books. He also writes illustrated storybooks for children (K-3) in the series <u>Stories for the Early Years</u>. Dr. Cohen holds three degrees in the physical sciences from the University of Wisconsin – Madison. During the course of his 45-year career he worked as an engineer, scientist, CBS Radio Station News Service (RSNS) commentator, private investigator, and Antarctic explorer. What he's been able to do with his background is mix fiction with reality in ways that even his family and friends have been unable to unravel!

Dr. Cohen's writings (he holds three degrees in the physical sciences from the University of Wisconsin – Madison) have received the highest reviews from Feathered Quill, Hollywood Book Reviews, Kirkus Discoveries, Pacific Book Review, Reader Views, and Readers' Favorite, among others, with many of his books recognized for their excellence through medals awarded by several of these same organizations following their annual book competitions. In 2017, for example, Readers' Favorite awarded Dr. Cohen's first short story anthology, *The Road Less Taken: A Collection of* Unusual *Short Stories - Book 1*, a Silver Medal while the National Association of Book Entrepreneurs (NABE) awarded the same book its Pinnacle Book Achievement Award for Best in Category: Short Stories. A member of the Society of Children's Book Writers and Illustrators (SCBWI), Dr. Cohen's articles often can be found in that organization's *BULLETIN* as well as in *Story Monsters Ink* magazine.

From December 1961 through early March 1962, Dr. Cohen participated in the 16th Chilean Expedition to the Antarctic. The US Board of Geographic Names in October, 1964, named the geographical feature Cohen Islands, located at 63° 18' S. latitude, 57° 53' W. longitude in the Cape Legoupil area, Antarctica, in his honor. And given he is an avid communicator (Dr. Cohen has been a licensed Radio Amateur since 1952, and holds an Amateur Extra Class license (call sign: N4XX)) and an accomplished violinist (he played with the Bryn Athyn (PA) Orchestra from 2007 through 2013), it is not unexpected that stories involving the Antarctic, radio, and music are to be found throughout his writings.

In addition to his adult and childrens books, Dr. Cohen writes Young Adult (YA) novels under the pen name Alyssa Devine. His YA novel *The Hypnotist* (Lexile® measure 930L) currently is in the Core Genre (Mystery) Reading Program at Neshaminy High School in Bucks County, Pennsylvania, where he is a guest lecturer on the subject of mystery writing.

Finally, from March 1966, through March, 1968, Dr. Cohen served as a Captain in the United States Army, Corps of Engineers.

Dr. Cohen lives in southeastern Pennsylvania, not far from where Washington crossed the Delaware River to surprise the Hessian forces in Trenton, New Jersey, on the night of December 25-26, 1776. Visit Ted at <www.theodore-cohen-novels.com>.

■ *Theodore Jerome Cohen*

www.ingramcontent.com/pod-product-compliance
Lightning Source LLC
Chambersburg PA
CBHW071943170626
46813CB00005B/1805